Once in a Blue Moon

Susan E Kirby

WIN

A CD MICRO-SYSTEM

■ *sapling*

First published in the UK in 1996 by Sapling, an imprint of
Boxtree Limited, Broadwall House, 21 Broadwall, London, SE1 9PL.

Published by arrangement with The Berkley Publishing Group,
a division of The Putnam Berkley Group, Inc., New York.

ISBN: 0 7522 0251 0

Printed and bound in Great Britain by
Cox & Wyman Ltd., Reading, Berkshire.

A catalogue record is available from the British Library.

Chapter 1

'Last day of school. Early dismissal. Sally and I are going to Truckers' Plaza to fill out applications. Haven't mentioned the job thing yet to Mom and Dad. Georgia's going to drive us since Michael can't be bothered.'

Two months ago, on Deanna Findley's sixteenth birthday, her mother had given her as a special gift the diary kept by her great-great-great grand-mother, Prudence Morris Hickman. 'Pru', as she was known to the family, had in her sixteenth year traveled the Overland Trail west to the Oregon Territory in 1852. Her diary was a record of the journey. Though Dee's own life seemed dull by comparison, the journal had inspired her to keep one of her own.

Hearing the screen door slam next door, she lifted her head from her spiral notebook. The scent of lilacs drifted on the air and floated through the bay window. She crossed to the second window, the one facing Michael McKinsey's house. Mayfield, a bustling central Illinois community of 30,000, was a far cry from the covered wagon train of Pru's day. The houses in their neighbourhood were comfortable ranch-style homes built on lots that were deep, but closely spaced. Except for a few low-hanging limbs of a red maple tree, she had an unobstructed view of Michael's grandfather, still in his pajamas, fumbling with his hat. Dee returned to the window-seat, leafed back the pages the breeze had turned and scribbled one last thought: 'What's with Michael, anyway?'

Michael was a senior, one year older than she. But they'd always been good friends. Or so she thought. Still feeling the sting of yesterday's rebuff, Dee turned up the sleeves of her jade green shirt, picked a thread off her white leggings and wished she hadn't asked Michael if he'd drive her and Sally out to the truck shop this afternoon. 'Give me a break, Dee. I've got stuff to do,' she mimicked in the mirror. It wasn't just the one incident, it was his whole attitude. He hadn't given her a lift to school in over a week. And twice now, he'd passed her in the halls without speaking. Could it be that girl from nearby Stevenson High? That Cheryl person he'd been dating? Maybe she had a jealous bone. Or maybe. . .

Enough, already! Changing her focus, Dee kicked a dirty sock over to her sister's side of the room and banged on the bathroom wall. 'Alice? Are you about done in there?'

'Chill, would you! I'm working on a lasting impression,' Alice called back.

'Troll!' Dee muttered in exasperation. She

moved the free-standing mirror in front of the window-seat, grabbed a comb from the walnut dressing-table, and sat down to French-braid her hair. It added a bit of style to what she considered an otherwise 'average' appearance. The mirror, like the dresser, was 'on loan' from Granny's Attic, her mother's antique shop. The glass was old and wavy and turned her gray eyes green. But what with Alice's marathon baths and her seven-year-old brother, Doug, scrubbing his rocks and bottles and miscellaneous relics, she had her choice of the mirror or trekking all the way downstairs to the basement bathroom.

'Dee?' Doug called from the hallway.

'Door's open.'

Doug was wearing a school shirt over his pajama bottoms. It was, Dee suspected, his wordless boast of another dry-night. 'Good for you!' she thought, anxious for him to overcome his bed-wetting problem. But she doubted he was going to stay dry, for he'd filled to the brim the copper tea kettle Mom found at an estate sale just last week. He flicked his tongue over a milk moustache as he crept on careful steps, then poured water into the rose-bowl holding an old corsage. Mr Kolupa, Michael's grandfather, had moved in next door just a little over a week ago. Paula McKinsey, Michael's mother, let Doug look through Mr Kolupa's cast-offs which she'd boxed up for Good Will. Doug was as sweet as the Sugar Pop stuck to his shirt. But his taste ran more to trash than treasures. He'd chosen

3

a pocket watch with a broken face, a Singer Sewing Machine medallion on a chain of old keys, and a mouldy book with a corsage pressed between its pages. He'd put the corsage in a rose-bowl and brought it to her room.

'You know dried flowers won't grow, don't you?' she said, just in case.

'They're dusty. They need a bath.'

'Careful,' she cautioned as the water-level climbed.

Being careful and being seven weren't compatible. Dee waited until he'd left with the teapot to wipe up after him. He was back moments later, fully dressed, the key-chain dangling from a belt loop. He perched on his knees on the window-seat, smudging the glass with his nose.

'Mr Kolupa is feeding the birds.'

'Is Michael with him?'

'No.'

Dee turned in the window-seat. The brim of Mr Kolupa's felt hat shadowed his seamed face as he wandered past Mom's lilac bush. She couldn't see that he had any bread crusts, but he was walking along, flinging his arm like he did.

'He's in our yard,' said Doug, moving away from the window.

'He isn't hurting anything.'

'Alice says he's loony.'

'Like Alice would know. He's forgetful, that's all.'

Doug's brow furrowed beneath his fringe of auburn hair.

4

'Mr Kolupa's a nice old guy, Doug,' Dee insisted. 'Michael and I used to play at his shop. He'd give us fabric scraps and let us sew on this old machine you had to pedal. Treadle, that's what they used before electric sewing-machines.'

'What else did you do?'

Dee smiled, remembering. 'One night a week, Mr Kolupa sprinkled sweeping compound all over the hardwood floor in the front room of his shop. He gave us each a quarter to sweep and set up the chairs.'

'For company?'

'No, prayer meeting,' said Dee. 'Just a few old people came.'

'Did you sit with them?' asked Doug.

'I usually went home before they came. But once, I remember sneaking upstairs with Michael and spying on them through a black grate in the floor.' Dee recalled ancient fans whirring and thin brittle voices harmonizing and Mr Kolupa praising and preaching and mopping his face with a bright red bandana. At the end of the service, they'd all gotten down on their knees facing the chairs. She'd whispered, 'Why are they smelling the chairs?' Michael'd laughed until an elderly lady had thrust her umbrella toward the ceiling, hissing, 'You little demons get away from that grate!'

Dee smiled in looking back, then quickly sobered, the sharpness of memories making her all the more indignant with Michael's recent distance.

He used to be so much fun, but that sure wasn't the case lately!

'Alice says he puts all the patio chairs in a circle,' Doug confided.

'There's no harm in that.'

'He talks to them,' Doug turned, plaintive voice insisting,

'Why would he do that, Dee?'

Dee dodged the question. 'Alice is a pain. You don't want to be a pain, do you?'

Doug fingered the gap left by a missing baby tooth and shook his head 'no'.

'Then be polite and cut Mr Kolupa some slack. Okay?'

'Okay.'

Deanna patted his shoulder. 'You're a good scout. Sit still. I'll comb your hair.'

Doug fingered the Singer medallion while Dee tried to tame his thick coarse waves. He looked out the window and asked with furrowed brow, 'Is Mr Kolupa an antique?'

'Definitely. But it isn't polite to say so.' Dee plucked the piece of sugar-coated cereal off his shirt and mused, 'You know, I'll bet this stuff would be good served over ice-cream with honey and nuts.'

Alice waltzed in draped in a towel. Alice was thirteen, and four years behind Dee in school, though who'd guess by looking? She was slim, moderately tall, nicely curved and wore her hair long like Dee. But the similarities ended there.

6

Dee had autumn-coloring – auburn hair, gray eyes, skin that darkened at the least hint of sun. Alice was blonde, blue-eyed, fair-complexioned and more generously curved than Dee. She reminded her sister of walking, talking mischief in Barbie doll wrappings as she held on to the towel with one hand and patted Doug on the head with the other.

'I told Mom not to put a lima bean sandwich in your lunch, but does she listen?'

'Lima beans! I hate lima beans.' Doug bolted out the door.

'You could have just asked him to leave,' said Dee dryly.

'What fun would that be?' Alice flashed a perfect white smile, dropped her towel and spilled a stack of clothes off her dresser in pursuit of clean undies.

Had Pru found her sisters as annoying as I find Alice? Wondering, Dee leaned toward the old wicker basket in the corner and mixed her spiral notebook in with a stack of identical notebooks. They were old school notebooks, mostly, though a couple were filled with poems and Dee's original recipes. Alice, who had neither culinary nor literary leanings, was so wrapped up in herself, she hadn't a clue Dee was keeping a journal. That made 'plain view' about the safest hiding place in their bedroom. Even then, Dee was fairly careful about what she recorded. You just never knew what mischief lurked in the heart of Alice.

Deanna left for school early, lest Michael get

the mistaken idea she was waiting around, hoping he'd offer her a ride. But when she got to the corner, Mr Kolupa stood at the curb watching the cars trickle out of their middle-call neighbourhood on to Virginia Boulevard. Had he lost weight, or was it the pajamas? He looked frail and restless and bewildered as he shifted from foot to foot. She hesitated a moment, feeling uneasy.

'Are you going somewhere, Mr Kolupa?'

His watery gaze shifted from her to the street and back again. He winced at a blaring horn and said, 'It's in Oklahoma.'

'You're going on a trip? That should be nice.'

'What?'

'I said that should be nice. Do you have friends there?'

'What?'

'Your trip to Oklahoma should be nice.'

'Out there where those things. . . those red things. . . they're low, not so tall. . . those dirt things.'

Dee's discomfort grew as he fumbled for words she couldn't guess. When he paused for breath, she inserted, 'The street's kind of busy this time of day. I'll walk you back, if you like.'

Mr Kolupa gripped the brim of his hat with one hand and wagged his head 'no'. He fumbled in his pajama pocket a moment, then looked at her more sharply. 'Have you seen my watch?'

'No, Mr Kolupa. I'm sorry, I haven't.'

Mr Kolupa's hands fluttered. 'Where is the

time? I'll miss the. . . it's going to go. . . it takes you. . . it goes right by. . .'

'The bus?' she guessed.

'Yes! I'm taking the bus home.'

There was relief in Mr Kolupa's voice as he said the words, as if he'd just now remembered why he was on the corner. He'd already missed the bus, though. There wouldn't be another one for an hour. *Did he really think he was going home? Why wasn't he dressed?* Wondering if she should intervene, and if so, how, Dee was relieved to see Michael dashing up the walk toward them. Shirtless and bare-footed, wearing nothing but cut-off sweatpants, he looked as if he'd thrown back the covers and come running. He slowed his steps as he drew closer. His blue gaze skipped over hers without quite meeting.

Dee kept her voice low. 'He wants to go home.'

'Yeah, I know. Thanks, Dee. I'll take it from here.' Fresh color stained cheeks still flushed from sleep. Appearing to deliberate his next move, Michael ran a hand over sandy hair. It was close-clipped except for a short fringe of curls at his neck.

Dee lingered. But the stiffness of Michael's shoulders, the tilt of his chin and the distance in his eyes relieved her of further involvement. Slim and fit, he towered over his grandfather. He moved slow and he didn't use size or strength, rather a gentle, if somewhat strained manner as he offered his grandfather his arm.

'Where were you? I looked for you,' the old man scolded.

'I overslept, Grandpa. But I'm here now,' Michael said quietly. 'Let's go home.'

'Home, yes. Let's go home, Richard.'

'Everything's fine. It's only a block. Here, hold on to my arm.' Michael kept on in the same reassuring tone, until finally Mr Kolupa took his arm and let Michael turn his around.

Richard? Dee thought as she watched their slow retreat past the trees and houses lining the street. Throwing non-existent crusts for the birds was harmless. As was wandering to the corner in your pajamas. But it wasn't normal. Maybe Alice was right after all. Maybe Mr Kolupa *had* lost his grip.

Water fights were tradition on the last day of school at Mayfield High. Kids packing squirt guns and selzer bottles milled about on the grass in front of the main doors. But Dee made it inside without incident.

Classes were all shortened because of early dismissal, so the day went pretty fast. PE was her last class and wouldn't you know? Tulip Johnson uncapped a bottle of cheap cologne and let fly, taking casualties, Dee among them. The other girls squealed and whined and lit into Tulip. Big-boned and audacious and prone to crazy stunts, Tulip enjoyed the attention. Dee refused to give her the satisfaction of getting annoyed. She washed the stuff off as best she could, then dashed out of the locker-room the moment the bell rang. Her friend

Sally Simmons was waiting for her in the corridor.

'Phew. What *is* that?' twanged Sally, wrinkling her freckled nose.

Dee rolled her eyes. 'Tulip Johnson made like an irrigation system with a bottle of cologne.'

Sally shook dark curls over her shoulder and drawled. 'That Tulip's a hoot. Introduce her to Mr Kolupa, why don't you? They can go on the road as a lawn-sprinkling, bird-feeding act.'

'Shh!' Dee warned, for they were nearing Michael's locker.

Looking injured, Sally said, 'It was just a joke.'

Hurriedly, Dee scanned the bodies choking the corridor and was relieved that Michael wasn't among them. Anxiety receding, she confided, 'I've got a feeling Michael's upset over his grandfather. I don't want him to think I've been spreading stories.' Dee pressed against Sally, trying to avoid being run over by a drove of shrieking water-pistol-wielding freshmen. 'How'd you know about that bird thing, anyway?'

'Alice told Yolanda at the lunch table.'

'Oh, great! So now everyone knows.'

'They're thirteen, Dee. Who listens?'

Alice's giggly friends. Dee heaved a sigh. 'I've said it before – Alice is not really my sister. She was left under the overpass by trolls.'

'Young, upwardly mobile trolls with good genes.' Sally shifted her book bag to the other arm.

'That's just a front for her friends.'

'A convincing one, at that,' Sally sighed and

11

added, 'With her looks, I'll bet she never has to go begging a job at a truck stop.'

'Think of it as an adventure. Anyway, we aren't begging, we're applying,' said Dee, looking forward to landing her first real job. She was torn between positions, though. Waitresses at Truckers' Plaza made more money than cooks because of tips. On the other hand, she might get a chance to show off her knack for garnishes, sauces, canapés and such if she worked in the kitchen. She said as much to Sally, hoping for some input.

'Even if you get a cook job, they won't let you monkey with the menu,' said Sally.

'You don't think so?'

'Course not. Go for the money,' advised Sally who had past experience in restaurant work. Spotting Georgia, she lunged down the hall. 'Georgia! Hey, Georgia! Wait up!'

Georgia motioned, grinning widely. 'Hurry up, Dee. Water fight's at Memorial Park. I've got a bucket full of water balloons in my trunk.'

Catching up, Dee reminded, 'We were counting on you to run us out to Truckers' Plaza.'

'I know. I'll drive you out, do the water fight thing, then come for you.'

Deanna had split ends longer than Georgia's memory. 'You won't forget?'

'Got it covered.' Georgia raced out the door and across the parking lot to the old beater her folks had bought for her. She got her foot in it, whittling the ten-minute drive to Truckers' Plaza down to seven and a half.

Dee's stomach flip-flopped as she and Sally climbed out and angled toward the truck stop entrance. The waitresses wore western shirts and jeans and cowboy boots. She heard change jingling in the pockets of their denim aprons as they swept past. If Sally was right, and they wouldn't let her experiment in the kitchen, she might just as well go for the money.

Sally exchanged glances with her and whispered, 'I hear the tighter your jeans, the better the tips.'

Guessing her source, Dee smothered a grin and whispered back, 'Yeah, and your brother Carl's the Donald Trump of the Plaza, I'll bet.'

'That tightwad? Get real!'

Deanna smothered her grin before following Sally up to the fuel desk to ask for job applications. They trekked down to the restaurant and filled them out over sodas and French fries. It took Sally a little longer, as Dee's only past experience had been babysitting. Upon their return, the clerk took their applications and said they could expect to hear in a week or so.

Deanna poked around in the gift shop while Sally made a pit stop. They left the building together just as Georgia pulled on to the gas island. She hopped out and squeezed the water from her pale gold hair before unscrewing the gas cap from her car. Her wet T-shirt and shorts clung like a second skin.

'How'd it go?' Georgia tossed a question their way as the pump kicked on.

'Not bad,' said Dee, feeling hopeful.

Sally filled in the details as Georgia pumped five dollars' worth into the tank. Dee made a contribution, then asked as they were leaving, 'How was the water fight?'

Georgia grinned cheerfully. 'Wet and wild. Your brother Carl's got it down to a science, Sal.'

'The empty fire extinguishers?' asked Sally.

'Empty, my eye!'

Sally grinned and filled Dee in. 'Carl and his pals got their hands on a couple of empty fire extinguishers. They pumped them full of water and compressed air.

'The cutting edge of water fights!' Georgia laughed. 'Tulip drove them through the park in her jeep and right down the sidewalk after Chisel Parker. He dived under a picnic table, and they still managed to drench him. Like an idiot, I fling a water balloon after them, and on the next lap, they got me.'

Georgia wove in and out of traffic with sophomoric skill, and kept up such a lively blow-by-blow of the water war, Dee regretted having missed it.

'Maybe you can talk Carl into letting you take one of those extinguishers with you to camp this summer,' suggested Sally.

Georgia bobbed her head, 'Negotiations are underway. *This year*, I'll be ready for those little scamps. They dumped me out of a canoe into the lake last summer, did I tell you?'

'You may have mentioned it.'

Deanna acknowledged Sally's wink with a smile. Last year was Georgia's first year as a counselor at summer camp. By her own admission, the kids had taken advantage of her good nature. 'When are you leaving?'

'I've got a couple of weeks yet.'

'Gonna miss you.'

'Ditto.' All at once, Georgia's hand flew to her head. 'Oh! I almost forgot to tell you! While we were at the park, some old guy swiped the flag from the veterans' monument.'

'You're kidding!' Dee exclaimed.

'Anyone try to stop him?' asked Dee.

'No. But Chisel threw a water balloon as he was walking away. Caught him right in the back. The old guy squealed and took on so. . .' Georgia's face clouded. 'There for a second, kind of put the damper on things.'

'What's "damper" than drenched?' quipped Sally.

'You really want to know?' Twinkle returning, Georgia whipped a water pistol from beneath the seat and nailed them both.

Chapter 2

'Grandpa got away from me this morning. I don't know if the move has added to his confusion, or if he's worse than we realized. By the time I got him calmed down and dressed and ready to go to Aunt Sheri's, it was so late, I ditched school and came home. Guess I can clean out my locker tonight.'

Michael scanned the words on the monitor. His father'd bought him his first computer just weeks before he was killed in a traffic accident ten years ago. He'd fantasized about a big computer terminal in the sky through which he could talk to Dad. Back then, he hadn't saved his entries, and he told no one, not even Grandpa Kolupa. Widowed just months before, Grandpa filled the loss in his life with Michael. They spent a lot of time together while Mom worked at the County Clerk's office at the Courthouse, just a block down from Grandpa's shop. Grandpa'd nurtured Michael, physically, emotionally and spiritually, and in time, largely because of Grandpa's influence, Michael's 'chats with Dad' became 'chats with God'. He saved them these days, and occasionally looked back through the entries. It fortified him to see that God had a way of working things out. So far, though, there'd been no resolution to the turmoil over Grandpa. Rather, the problems were intensifying as time went on.

Grandpa called me 'Richard' again. Just my luck he'd say it in front of Dee. It pushed her pity button, I could tell. Too bad I'm not looking for sympathy.'

He hesitated, uncomfortable saying what he did want from Dee. Was it hot in here or what? Michael wandered out to the kitchen and popped the top of a can of soda, thinking of Dee's rich auburn hair and long slim legs. She had great eyes, too. They were gray and green and a little gold, depending on light and shadow. It was like looking into a marble, only a lot more intriguing. The phone put the skids on a familiar daydream of mutual attraction. It was his mother, calling from work.

'Michael! Thank goodness I got you!' her harried voice brought every nerve to attention.

'What's the matter?'

'Dad got away from Sheri and walked all the way to Memorial Park. Bill. . .'

'Got away?' Soda fizzed over Michael's hand as his grip on the soft aluminum can tightened. 'How?'

'Sheri was in the kitchen with the kids. Dad simply walked away.'

'But she found him, right?'

'Yes, he's fine,' his mother curbed the stress-running-amuck in her voice. 'He took the flag from the veterans' memorial. Someone called the police.'

'Oh, great!'

'No, it's okay. Bill Buckley took the call. He saw it was Dad, realized what'd happened and got in touch with me here at the Courthouse.'

'Is he bringing Grandpa home?'

'He intended to. But Dad was upset by the police car and didn't want to get in. Bill put him in a cab. He was sweet about it. Said his wife's sister's mother-in-law had some kind of dementia, too.'

As in demented. Michael winced at the word and muttered, 'Is that supposed to make us feel better?'

'People mean well. No point in being thin-skinned.'

He sipped his soda and weathered her mild reproof. 'What about Aunt Sheri?'

'She's upset, of course, and feeling guilty for letting him get away, and at the same time, a little sorry for herself. I guess I would too, in her shoes.'

Forty-one, two toddlers underfoot and a third child due soon? Michael sympathized, remembering how he'd freaked when Grandpa'd gotten away from him this morning.'

'There's change in my jewelry box to cover the fare,' his mother was saying.

'He'll settle down soon surely.'

'I hope so. I feel badly, dumping this on you.'

19

'You aren't dumping, I offered,' he reminded.

'My hero!' she said with a smile in her voice. 'By the way, the cleaners promised to have your graduation gown pressed by five. I'll pick it up on my way home. Aunt Sheri's still planning on coming over to stay with Dad. Walt will be home to watch the kids. I told her we could take Dad with us if she wanted to see you graduate. But she says her feet are too swollen for dress shoes, and that all the commotion would be hard on Dad anyway.'

'I'd skip myself if it weren't for you and your fresh roll of film.'

'Don't even think about it! You're working on your valedictorian speech, aren't you?'

He chuckled, his academic achievement somewhat more modest. 'A diploma will do nicely.'

'I still say we should have planned a party.'

'Mom, don't start.'

'Okay, okay. I just want you to know I'm proud of your hard work. Speaking of which, I'd better get back. Real estate bills went out yesterday and taxpayers are whining.'

'Is *that* what it is? Thought it was Aunt Sheri, going into labor.'

'Later, smarty.'

Joking aside, Michael was relieved that after what'd happened, Aunt Sheri was still planning on staying with Grandpa tonight. Grandpa's sickness was a private matter, and he didn't want to be put in the position of having to make explanations to friends. What were they going to do, though, once

20

Aunt Sheri's baby came? They'd have no back-up at all.

Hearing the cab turn in the drive, Michael shut down his computer. He paid the driver. His grandfather made no attempt to get out. The veins in his hands were plumped up like cooked spaghetti as he sat smoothing the crumbled flag in his lap.

Michael leaned into the back seat. 'You're home, Grandpa. Climb out.'

'I have to... where's the? It's...loose,' said Grandpa, fingers plucking at the wind-frayed ends of the flag. Michael's nerves tightened at the cab-bie's curious glance. 'Come inside, Grandpa. I'll help you sew it.'

Mr Kolupa accepted Michael's hand out. But he balked at the edge of the sidewalk. 'This isn't the place. Let's go home.'

'It's okay. We'll go inside. You can sit down and rest.' Michael put a hand on the small of his back and urged him toward the door. 'How'd your shirt get wet?'

Grandpa held out a hand, palm up and said with a touch of impatience, 'It's raining, Richard.'

'We better hustle then, before we get wet,' said Michael, though it wasn't raining and his great-uncle Richard had been dead for fifty years.

Grandpa Kolupa offered no resistance. He will-ingly traded the damp shirt for a dry one, but couldn't remember if he'd eaten lunch. Michael settled him in the kitchen, poured a glass of juice and fixed a snack just in case. Grandpa bowed his head as was his custom.

'My grace is sufficient for thee,' he said instead of giving thanks. Then he sat, looking puzzled.

'Amen,' said Michael.

Grandpa nodded and picked up his fork, as if the word had freed him. He ate quickly and not too neatly, then went to his room, stretched out on the bed and soon dozed off.

Michael put the dishes into the dishwasher and picked up the flag Grandpa'd left on the bench in the foyer. Flag-mending had been a small part of his grandfather's tailoring business and simple enough he'd continued to care for a number of flags around town long after he'd retired. But he'd given that up too, after a bout with the flu two winters ago that'd left him weak and more absent-minded than ever. Concerns about Grandpa's health and safety had resulted in Mom and Aunt Sheri putting him in the Senior Care Center, where he had two hot meals and supervision all day long. A bus picked him up in the morning and dropped him off at his building late in the afternoon. Mom or Aunt Sheri or Michael checked on him twice a day, either by phone or in person. That'd worked very well, until Grandpa began wandering away from the Senior Care Center. Two weeks ago, when he'd wandered off, he'd gotten lost just blocks from the building that'd been his home and his work place for decades. Michael'd come home from school to learn that the Center would no longer take him because of his wandering. Aunt Sheri was there. She and Mom were talking about moving Grandpa into a nursing home. Certain that was no place for his grandfather, Michael reminded Mom of all the ways Grandpa had been there for *them*.

'We don't feel good about this either,' said Aunt Sheri. 'But what other option do we have?'

'I'll take care of him.' The words flew out of his mouth.

Mom protested it was too much, that Grandpa wouldn't want him giving up his summer.

'Besides, you have no experience. You couldn't begin to manage!' argued Aunt Sheri.

Grandpa's doctor tried to discourage him too, explaining the difficulties of tending someone with a dementing illness. Tenacity, however, had prevailed and Mom and Aunt Sheri had agreed to let him try.

'But it's just for the summer,' Mom added.

So they moved Grandpa in. With just a few days of classes remaining, Michael took care of him before and after school, Aunt Sheri during the day. Now that school was out, he'd be taking full responsibility. And though he wouldn't admit it, not even to Mom, his confidence in his ability to cope had suffered some blows over the past week and a half. He hoped the doctor was right, and that with a calm environment and established routines, Grandpa would eventually settle down from the upset of the move.

Welcoming some time alone, Michael picked up a book on neon. Neon signs were gaining popularity again. The more he read about neon, the more fascinated he became with it, both as an art form and as an advertising technique. Interest taking a practical turn, he wanted to learn how to make the gas-filled signs, then established his own business, supplying local businesses with custom-made neon signs. It was hard to concentrate though, with Alice next door teasing Doug.

'He's a bloody old boogedy head and those keys unlock his dungeon,' her voice drifted through the open window. 'He'll lock you up, cut you into little pieces and sprinkle you on the grass for the birds!'

'That's not so, you're making it up,' Doug retorted.

'Just remember, I warned you.'

'I'm not scared, cause you're lying.'

'Okay, wed-better.'

'You're not supposed to say that. I'm telling Dee!'

A door slammed, and the next thing Michael heard was Deanna hollering at Alice to mow the yard if she couldn't find anything better to do than tease Doug.

'You're suppose to do it. That was the deal when I loaned you the money,' Alice protested.

'Deal's off. Do your own mowing.'

'I want my money, then.'

The door slammed again. Michael crossed to the window. Dee'd gone back inside. But she must have been peering out, for Alice hollered, 'I'm charging you a dollar a day interest, starting right now!'

Yep. Definitely summertime at the Findley household.

Counting on Grandpa sleeping a while, Michael slipped out to the garage to change the oil in his truck. A '66 Ford, the pickup had belonged to Grandpa Kolupa. The body, styled with front-fender bulges, could use some bonding and a paint job. But the engine had been well maintained over the years. Michael kept the truck tuned, burning clean, and immaculate inside and out. It was stuffy in the garage and the light wasn't all that great, so he backed the truck out and drove across the grass to the other end of the house. The big maple tree between his house and Dee's provided a nice patch of shade, plus Grandpa's bedroom window was just a few strides away.

Michael was putting a pan beneath it to catch the old oil when the lawn-mower started up next door. Would it wake Grandpa? Not taking any chances, he pulled the oil plug, left the oil draining and dashed indoors to close the bedroom window.

Grandpa was sleeping soundly, his bed in plain view of the window. Quietly, Michael opened the curtains a crack so he could keep an eye on him from outdoors. After a moment's deliberation, he blocked the front door with a heavy chair, then pushed the kitchen table in front of the back door. That left only the door leading from the kitchen into the garage. That was solved easily enough – he closed the automatic overhead door. Even if Grandpa found the switch on the wall, he'd hear the door open and catch up with Grandpa before he had a chance to wander away.

With all the precautions in place, the oil change went pretty smoothly. Michael was wrapping it up when the mower made a pass along the unmarked lot line between his yard and the Findleys'. Stretched out on his back beneath the truck, he caught a glimpse of grass-stained sneakers slapping along after the mower. The third pass came a little too close, shooting grass all over him.

'Alice!' He slid out, spitting clippings, only to realize the legs attached to those sneakers belonged to Dee, not her sister. He raised his voice to be heard over the mower.

'Throttle it up, Dee. Maybe you can nail the poodle across the street.'

She cupped a hand to her ear, indicating she hadn't understood a word he'd said, and throttled down the mower. 'Problem with the truck?'

'No. Just changing the oil.' *With the lawn stretching out behind her, her eyes were green.* He got to his feet and propped a sneaker on the chrome side-iron of his truck, asking, as he tied dragging laces, 'What gives? I thought it was Alice's turn to mow.'

Dee wrinkled her nose. 'Alice is an opportunist.'

He grinned. 'And you're encouraging her?'

'Did I mention money changed hands?'

'Pays good, does she?'

'Loan sharking is more her line. But hopefully, Truckers' Plaza will call me in a few days.'

'That was today, wasn't it? How'd it go?'

'Well enough to take me away from all this, I hope.'

She swept an arm across her damp brow, shut off the mower, and closed the remaining distance between them, exclaiming, 'Shade feels pretty good.'

'Doesn't it, though?'

Her face was flushed and shiny, her perfume heat-radiated. She nudged his foot off the side iron and sat down to dust grass clippings off her slender ankles. 'I don't think I can take another summer of being in charge,' she confided. 'How about you? That muffler and lube place call you?'

'I decided to hang out with Grandpa instead.' Seeing her expression soften, he skipped quickly to another topic. 'Get school shut down without me, did they?'

'Guess so. I noticed you weren't there. You're going to graduation, aren't you?'

'According to Mom, I am.'

'Is there a bash afterwards?'

'Mom offered, but you gotta draw the line somewhere. Besides, I've been invited to half a dozen parties.'

'Sounds like you're booked, then.' She smiled. 'Maybe I'll give you your present now.'

'You got me something?'

'Sure, what'd you think?'

He'd been too preoccupied with Grandpa to give it any thought. But presents were nice, unexpected or otherwise. Particularly from Dee.

Dee shot a playful look over her shoulder on her way to the house. She indicated the mower with a flick of her hand. 'Take that baby for a spin, why don't you? She's fully loaded. Convertible top. Cruise control, tilt seats, air and a disk player right there on the console. Can't put a price tag on that kind of luxury.'

Distracted by her smile, he was a little slow on the uptake. 'The lawn-mower, right?'

She dashed inside without answering, then came back with a brightly wrapped package. 'Careful. It's fragile.'

Michael peeled off the wrappings and pulled from the rectangular box a bright green neon sign. It was shaped in the outline of a car and lettered 'Mick's Autos'. Belatedly understanding her car sales pitch, he whistled low. 'Now here's a piece of work. Thanks, Dee.'

She shrugged modestly. 'Not quite *Mike*. But I figured you'd like it anyway, the way you get off on neon.'

'This is great.' He ran his hand along the curves and bends in the glass. 'Well-crafted and in good condition. Must have hung indoors out of the weather.' He reached in through the open window of his truck, grabbed the remote, and pointed it toward the garage at the opposite end of the house. The door lumbered open. Beckoning, he invited, 'Come on inside. We'll light it up.'

Dee accompanied him through the garage, then held the kitchen door for him. He saw her gaze skip over the table he'd pushed up against the back door. But she didn't comment or question.

'I bought it at a flea market. Dad says Mick's Autos used to be over on West Market.'

'It went belly up a couple of years ago.' Michael took a wreath of dried flowers off the kitchen wall and hung the sign in its place.

'Plug it in.'

Michael did so, then backed away, admiring the sign. 'You've got a gift for gifts, Dee. Thanks again.'

She cocked her head to one side, her gaze critical. 'There's too much light in here, though. Doesn't really do it justice. How about the pantry? No outside windows.'

Closed in the pantry with Dee and a neon light? Possibilities flickering, Michael was about to comply when he heard Grandpa shuffling in the next room. Apprehension crowded out his pleasure. Changing course, he pointed out, 'There's no outlet in there. Let's skip it for now. I'll hang it in the front window and plug it in tonight.'

'Whatever.'

Above and beyond anxious thoughts of his grandfather was that familiar stirring he got every time Dee came round. It was hard to know how to get beyond their long-standing friendship to unchartered territory. 'You coming tonight?' he asked, walking her to the door.

'Graduation?' She nodded. 'I'm passing out programs.'

'I'll give you a lift if you don't mind going a little early. I have to clean out my locker.'

'Sure, that'd be fine.'

'I'll pick up my diploma, shake a few hands and we're outta there.' He pushed the screen door open and held it with one hand. 'Soon as it's dark, we'll cruise by here and check out "Mick's Autos".'

'Sounds good.'

Impulsively, he added, 'We can drop in on a couple of parties, too. If you want to, that is.'

'Is that what you want?'

Sensitive to nuance, he asked, 'What's that supposed to mean?'

There was a fly on the other side of the screen door. She flicked at it, not quite meeting his gaze. 'Seems like you've been kind of busy lately.'

Busy wasn't her first choice, he could tell by the way she hesitated, then hurried the word on its way. It wasn't perfect, as openings go. Still, he considered seizing the moment. Telling her their old relationship didn't work for him anymore, could there be something more? But before he could find the words, Grandpa came in from the living-room. His suspenders were down and his pants were unzipped. Impulse squelched, Michael said, 'Don't keep that fully loaded mower waiting. Alice the loan shark'll send her thugs.'

Dee grinned and countered, 'I'd like to feed her to sharks.'

'Poor Alice.'

'Yeah, right,' she said, tone laced with sarcasm. But she dimpled, tossed her hand into the air and turned away.

Michael's gaze followed her through the garage. Good as she was with Doug, Dee'd kind of lost her handle on Alice the last couple of years. Alice was full of vinegar, as Grandpa would say. Crowding Dee, was she?

'Who was that, Richard?'

Aware of a faint throb just over his left eye, Michael hooked the screen and turned his attention to Grandpa.

Chapter 3

'Michael liked his present. Almost makes it worth being in to debt Alice. Dad set rafters today on the house his construction crew is building. He was hot and tired and in no mood, so I wasn't going to mention the job thing yet. But Alice, bless her fiendish heart, brought it up over dessert. Guess Yolanda told her. I would pick a friend whose sister's my sister's best friend. At any rate, I explained about putting in an application. Ever since Mom broke her foot, she's been anxious for school to be out so Alice can help her at the shop. But she wished me luck and said she'd adjust accordingly if I get the job. Dad's okay with it, too. Surprise, surprise. But not Doug. He doesn't want Alice being in charge of him. Who could blame the kid?'

Dee shifted on the porch swing and looked back over her shoulder at Michael's house. She should have asked him to be a bit more specific than 'early'. She'd been waiting out here on the porch for twenty minutes. Her neck was damp beneath the weight of her hair. She could feel the humidity beading her brow, wilting her curl and zapping the

33

starch from her white dress. Slipping out of stylish flats, Dee put pen to journal again.

'It's weird about Michael. This morning I thought he was avoiding me. This afternoon he offers me a lift to and from graduation, then asks if I want to go party-hopping. Guess he got caught without a date. Wonder if that means he's splitsville with that Cheryl person. Hope so. He can do better. He's cute and he's smart and he's kind. Like this morning when his grandfather wandered to the corner in his pee jays? He didn't raise his voice and he didn't correct Mr Kolupa even when he called him Richard. I wonder, who's Richard?'

'Dee? You ready to go?'

Dee looked up to find Michael at the bottom of the porch steps, looking sharp in a dark suit and tie nearly as blue as his eyes. She slapped her journal shut and jumped up. The swing recoiled and smacked into the back of her legs. A paint chip poked her leg through her nylons. She twisted, trying to examine the damage.

'Snagged! I better run in and change.'

'No time, Dee. Anyway, the dress is fine.'

'My hose, not my dress.'

'Oh.' Michael gave her the once-over and grinned. 'Those look fine too.'

Dee smiled and swept a hand in his direction. 'Nice suit.'

'Mom's idea. I was leaning toward something more casual,' Michael confessed, but he looked pleased at the compliment. He glanced at his watch as she tucked her journal into her oversized bag and slipped on her shoes.

'Cologne, no less,' said Dee, catching a spicy blend as she descended the steps. 'Are we late?'

'Starting to be,' said Michael, cutting across the grass at her side. 'Aunt Sheri was going to come over. But Uncle Walt called to say she'd gone into labor and they were leaving for the hospital. We had to work out some stuff and it threw us behind.'

'I didn't think her baby was due for a couple of weeks.'

'That was Central Standard Doctor time. Apparently, no one told the baby.'

'Bet it's another girl.'

'Fifty-fifty chance of it.' He shot a distracted glance toward his house, then circled to her side to open the truck door. She smiled and ribbed. 'Michael! You've learned a new trick!'

'The door? That's how it's done on a date. Hadn't you heard?'

'This is a date?'

'I asked you out, you accepted. That's a date, isn't it?'

'I thought it was a lift.'

'Just get in.'

'I dunno. I'm starting to feel some pressure,' she joked, certain he wasn't serious.

'In that case, it's a lift.'

Dee let him close her in, but noticed, as he circled to the other side to climb behind the wheel, that his ears were red. It caught her up short. Was he serious? Had he really intended it to be a date? Dee settled her bag on floor-mats clean as a dinner plate and buckled her seat-belt as he backed out of the driveway. Suddenly self-conscious, she grabbed the first subject to come to mind, asking, 'How come your grandfather's taken to calling you Richard?'

'Richard was his brother. He was killed in the war.' Michael shifted gears and sped toward the corner without elaborating.

'Is there a family resemblance?'

'Between Richard and me? Judging by old photos, I've got to say no.'

'Funny he should call you that, then.'

Michael shrugged and offered no explanation as they waited to feed on to Virginia Avenue. Dee lifted her hair off her neck and let the breeze coming through the window cool it. The truck was old. But it idled quiet as a lullaby. The silence stretched as long and drab as the dark cap and gown on the seat between them. Dee picked up the cap and fiddled with the tassel. The silence was killing her.

'Was he a foot-soldier? Your Uncle Richard,' she prompted at his blank expression.

'Fighter pilot.' He reached out the window and adjusted the side mirror.

'How'd he die?' she asked.

'Shot down over France.'

'Were he and your grandfather close? Or more like Alice and me?'

'I'm not sure.'

'If he'd lived he'd be what. . .about seventy? Eighty?' She let the threads of the tassel sift through her fingers. 'Missing out on all those years. It's sad.'

'Yeah, when you think about it.' Michael found a hole in the traffic, and filled it.

That 'date' word, Dee decided, was fatal. It was like riding with a stranger. He adjusted the mirror, fidgeted with the sun visor, toyed with the radio dial. All in silence. The ride couldn't be over soon enough for her! She draped his gown over her arm and climbed out without waiting to see if he'd do the door thing again.

'I was supposed to be in the auditorium ten minutes ago. How about cleaning out my locker for me?'

Relieved to hear him initiate, Dee complained, 'You skip school and I get clean-up detail. That's real fair.'

Michael grinned and reached beneath the seat for an old gym bag. 'Just shove it all in here, okay?'

Deanna traded the cap and gown for the bag and committed his combination to memory. They parted company outside the auditorium where the rest of the seniors had gathered. She traveled two long corridors, worked his combo, then crammed a year's worth of pens, crumpled papers and worn folders into the gym bag. There wasn't room for his walkman, so she poked it into her pocketbook.

Dee ran the bag out to Michael's truck, then

37

returned to collect the programs she was supposed to hand out. A steady stream of family and friends filed into the gymnasium. The air-conditioning couldn't keep up with all that body heat. The programs, doubling as fans, went fast. By the time Michael's mother came through the door, Dee was nearly out. Mr Kolupa was with her. He was freshly shaven and neatly dressed in a suit and tie.

'Hello, Paula. Mr Kolupa. You're looking snappy.'

'Doesn't he though?' Paula smoothed down one point of his collar, then patted his hand. 'Dad, you remember Dee Findley, don't you? She lives next door. She and Michael are friends.'

Mr Kolupa gave her a vacant nod. Just a few feet away, the band began to play. They were lively but loud. The acoustics weren't that great in the gym. It must have hurt Mr Kolupa's ears. He wrestled his arm free of Paula's grip. 'Let's go home.'

'We just got here, Dad. We're going to see Michael graduate. Remember?'

Mr Kolupa turned back the way he'd come and shuffled into the corridor. Generously rounded and flushed from rushing, Paula thrust her camera and pocketbook at Dee. 'Be a dear, would you Dee, and hold my things while I get him?' Sheri's at the hospital and I couldn't find anyone else to stay with him.'

Dee couldn't hear from her place at the door what Michael's mother said to Mr Kolupa. But her manner, like Michael's, was patient and gentle. At

38

length, she managed to coax her father to return to the gym. The only remaining seats were in the back, close to the band. There was a path through the middle of the chairs for the graduating class's march to their seats of honor up front. Paula took the aisle seat in the back row and settled Mr Kolupa beside her. Following, Dee returned Paula's belongings just as the band launched into *Pomp and Circumstance*.

'Sit with us, if you'd like,' invited Paula. She indicated the chair to her father's left.

Sally's brother Carl and Georgia's cousin were also graduating. Sally and Georgia were saving Dee a top row seat. But the seniors were filing in, and she hated to climb the bleachers now that the audience was seated and quiet. 'Excusing' herself past Paula and Mr Kolupa, Dee sat down and dropped her bag on the floor in front of her.

The girls were wearing white caps and gowns and carrying red roses. It was a nice contrast to the boys' dark colors. Dee was checking out her program to see if the seniors were marching in in the order they were listed when Paula stood up to take a picture. Mr Kolupa grasped the back of the chair in front of him and pulled himself to his feet.

'Sit down, Dad,' urged Paula.

'Is it time to go?'

'No, I'm taking a picture.'

Wordlessly, Mr Kolupa reached for the camera. Paula dodged his hand. 'Thanks anyway, Dad, but I'll snap it. Sit down, please,' she added. But he was slow to do so. By the time she had her father back in his chair, Michael'd already passed by.

Deanna could see Paula was disappointed. As for Michael, he never missed a beat of his sedate march. But she knew from the way his ears caught fire that the camera incident hadn't escaped his attention. Being a fairly low-profile person herself, she empathized. The band played on and the long line of seniors began filling the chairs on the risers up front. When they were all seated, the music stopped. The president of the board of education spoke her welcome over the whisper of fanning papers. A minister gave a lengthy invocation. Beside her, Mr Kolupa rocked in his chair. He fidgeted with his hat. The valedictorian was at the podium beginning her speech when he put it on his head.

'Let's go,' he said.

'Not yet, Dad,' whispered Paula. She removed his hat, and put it in his lap.

He stroked the brim, the ribbon, the lining. He began tapping his feet. Dee saw Paula lay a quieting hand on one knee, but he kept tapping.

'Please, Dad. Sit still. You're disturbing the people around us,' she whispered.

He quieted for a minute, maybe two. Then he put his hat on again, and said, 'It's time to go home.'

Again, Paula quieted him. But people around them were stealing glances. Some looked annoyed at the disruption, some curious, others amused.

Dee wished she'd climbed the bleachers. Paula might as well have stayed home with her father. Michael's graduation was going on right before her eyes and she was missing it as she struggled to keep her father quiet.

Finally, they began reading names and passing out diplomas. They did it alphabetically. Mr Kolupa grew increasingly restless as they worked their way toward 'McKinsey'. Seeing Paula's attention shift to her camera, Dee braced herself for the inevitable. Sure enough, Michael's mother leaned past Mr Kolupa and said, 'I want a picture of Michael getting his diploma. Would you mind staying with Dad while I slip up front? I'll only be a moment.'

Deanna minded. She minded a lot. But what could she say? Forcing a strained smile, she motioned Paula on.

'Are we going?' asked Mr Kolupa.

'No, no! She's taking a picture, she'll be right back,' whispered Dee.

'What?'

'She's taking Michael's picture,' she said a little louder.

'What?'

He said it so loudly, the woman to Dee's left turned a cold stare on them both. Heat flooded Dee's cheeks. She reached into her purse for a roll of lifesavers and gave one to Mr Kolupa. It sounded like a rock slide as he crunched it between his teeth, then smacked his lips. At least he was still in his seat. She gave him another one. Then another. Heads turned a row in front of them, so she put the remaining lifesavers in her bag. Mr Kolupa stuck his hand in after them just as they called Michael's name.

'Michael's getting his diploma,' Dee tried to distract the old man from his candy caper. But he just kept digging in her purse. Flustered and uncertain what to do, she pulled, hoping to ease it away from him. But she had to quit when it looked like it was going to turn into a tug of war. Mr Kolupa's hat fell to the floor. He spilled her journal, her cosmetic bag and her hairbrush on top of it. But he hung on to Michael's walkman. He held it up and smiled.

'It's a. . .it makes. . .it sings.'

'Yes.' She nodded. 'You want to hear?'

'No,' he said. But there was a spark in his eyes that hadn't been there before.

Dee put on the headphones. She found an easy listening station, turned down the volume, and was about to take the big gamble when Paula returned.

Paula promptly took over with the headphones. 'Here, Dad. Listen!' She fit them to her father's ears.

The soft music appeared to calm Mr Kolupa. He began tapping his feet again, but gently, as if in time to the music. Red-faced and perspiring, Paula let him tap.

The last diploma was given out. The president of the board presented the Class of '95. A cheer went up from the audience. The seniors came down off the risers, flinging their caps into the air and showering one another in confetti. Friends clapped friends on the shoulder. Others hugged.

It must have looked like dancing to Mr Kolupa. He pushed his chair back and shuffled from foot to foot. His motions lacked grace and style and sent a buzz of amusement through the band just behind him. It *was* comical in a way. But sad too, that he should dance to music he alone heard while others looked on, holding back laughter. Heat prickled Dee's neck and washed over her face. She looked to Paula to make him stop as, behind them, the band struck up the recessional.

The audience swelled to their feet. They clapped in recognition of the graduates as they regrouped and began marching out. Mr Kolupa kept dancing. Paula, looking harassed and worn and faintly defiant, was poised for a final shot of Michael as he exited with his classmates. She made no attempt to rein in her father. Maybe she reasoned he wasn't hurting anyone. Or thought he'd go unnoticed, as people snapped photos and shook hands and tried to talk over the band.

Dee had no doubt that one person would notice. Wanting to spare Michael, she pulled the plug on the radio. Mr Kolupa ran down like a wind-up toy. He cocked his head on one side, listening for lost music as behind him the band played on.

Michael matched his classmates' hurried strides. Dee could tell he was glad it was over. Watching him, she felt an affinity for this friend from her sandbox days. Pride and affection, too. His blue gaze, as he passed, skimmed his motionless grandfather and met hers for the briefest of moments. The creases in his brow disappeared. He smiled and tossed her a red rose. The feeling in her stomach as she reached out to catch it made her forget all about Mr Kolupa. The cacophony of voices and instruments and milling people faded. What was this tenderness turning? This melting within? Was it the mood of the evening? The sentiment of well-trod paths coming to a close? Must be. She ducked her head, thinking fleetingly of Pru's diary entry on the day she'd left her hometown of sixteen years to embark on the journey of a lifetime.

'*I'm excited about going,*' she'd written. *But as I said good-bye and hugged each of my cousins in turn, I knew my life was about to change for ever. I couldn't decide if I was the happiest sad girl in these whole United States. Or the saddest happy girl.*'

Chapter 4

'For the past week, I've been out of sorts, thinking Michael was blowing me out because of that Cheryl person or because he was graduating or because he was moving on with his life. Now I'm not so sure. Could this date be real? The rose. The look. The smile. What does it all mean?'

'So here you are. I've looked all over for you!'

Deanna snapped her journal closed as Sally slid into the chair beside her. Paula and Mr Kolupa were gone. The band, too. The graduates were lined along the corridor beyond the gym shaking hands with wellwishers. With the chairs around her all empty, she'd opened her journal as she'd waited for Michael, and the words poured out.

'School's out, girl. You can quit with the extra credit.' Fishnet stockings swished as Sally dropped down beside her, crossed her legs and tugged at her skirt.

'Just scribbling.' Dee tucked her journal into her purse. 'Think of it, Sal. Another year and it'll be our turn.'

'None too soon.' Sally's glance skipped to the

red petals peeking out of the bag at Dee's feet. 'Where'd you get the rose?'

'Someone tossed it, I caught it.' Dee kept it simple, lest Sally misconstrue.

'Cool.' Sally tugged at her arm, pulling her to her feet. 'Come on. Georgia's waiting in the car. I promised Mom I'd beat her home and lay out the spread.'

'You two go on without me. Michael's giving me a lift,' Dee said quickly.

'Great! I'll see you both there.' Sally turned back, doubt rippling her brow. 'You *are* coming early, aren't you?'

'Do my best. Michael mentioned some other parties, too. He didn't say what order.'

'He's taking you on his rounds?' Sally's sparsely plucked brows climbed. 'Guess that means McKinsey's over his mood. What's he trying to do – make it up to you for being such a dweeb the last few days?'

'Something like that.'

'In that case, a buddy 'big brother' beats the real thing,' said Sally. 'I've been bugging Carl to let me tag along on his party hop. It's not like he has a date or anything. But you know Carl. He's pretending he doesn't know me.'

Deanna wasn't fooled. Sally and Carl were tight. She'd been knocking herself out, planning his graduation party for weeks.

'It's gonna be a blockbuster doings, Sal,' Dee said warmly. 'Hope he appreciates your efforts.'

'It was no big sacrifice.' Sally swept dark tresses back from her thin freckled features. 'He'll move on down the party circuit, and I'll end up hostessing the gig.'

'No doubt.' With so many families celebrating, graduation night was one long progressive house-to-house bash.

Sally raced off to catch up with Georgia while Dee joined the thinning ranks in the corridor beyond the gym. Michael fell out of line and came to meet her. They paused in the auditorium long enough for him to add his cap and gown to a growing pile.

It was a purple dusk with a gentle breeze stirring. Michael held the truck door for her once again. 'Up for some neon-sighting?' he asked as he tossed his diploma and a couple of cards in after her.

Deanna smiled. 'I hear there's a first-rate piece at Mick's on Ash Street.'

'You don't say.'

'It looks deceptively like the McKinsey house. But the sign says it's a car lot.'

'Signs don't lie,' he played along.

'Bad neighbourhood, though. This Mick character has been known to snitch roses from graduating girls. Then there's the loan shark who lives next door.'

'With her poor mistreated Cinderella sister?'

'You've heard this one?'

Michael laughed as he circled to the other side

and climbed in. Determined the mire of silence that'd enveloped them earlier would not suck them under again, Dee kept up the banter. Windows down, wind snatching words, they talked and laughed their way down Virginia Boulevard.

Michael's bedroom faced Ash Street. The bright green against the dark window was sensational. They sat admiring the sign from Michael's driveway. He killed the headlights and stretched his arm along the seat. 'Best graduation present yet.'

'And thank *you* for the rose.'

'I didn't snitch, I bartered.'

'I won't ask how.' Dee smiled and buried her nose in fragrant petals.

He nudged her shoulder. 'If you're planning on swimming at Trevor's, better suit up now. There'll be a mob at his place, and there's only one bathroom in the pool house.'

Dee ran home to change. Her suit was a shirred-bandeau one-piece, vividly floral and flattering to her slender curves. She tugged a short, lightweight sundress over it, slipped into sandals, and shoved a comb, a towel and clean undergarments into her beach bag.

Alice and Doug were watching TV. But her father'd gone to bed. Dee was quiet in the kitchen, finding a bud vase, running water. She carried it back to her room for her rose and noted, as she placed it on the dresser, that Doug's corsage had disintegrated. Her mother limped out of the bathroom with a plastic bag around her walking cast and granted her an extension on her midnight cur-few. The night was young. Life was good.

Michael hadn't returned to the truck. Dee mounted the front porch nearly identical to their own and dropped into a deckchair to wait. The windows were open. Voices drifted out, first Paula's, then Michael's asking how his grandfather had weathered graduation. Dee recognized depths to a seemingly casual question. She leaned for-ward, listening.

'Piece of cake,' Paula's reply was more reassur-ing than truthful. 'Dee was good with Dad.'

'I wish you hadn't asked her to sit with you.'

Paula didn't bother wedging a denial into the slight pause.

'Let's keep this between us, okay?'

'There's no reason to be embarrassed,' his mother reasoned.

'I'm not. I just don't think it's anyone's business.'

Dee winced at his tone, but kept listening.

'We're going to need other people from time to time, Michael,' Paula was saying. 'When we start building walls, we become prisoners of our cir-cumstances. I don't want to live like that, and I don't think you do, either.'

'Spare me the group therapy mumbo-jumbo.'

'It isn't therapy, it's a support group. I wish you'd come with me just once. In case you haven't realized it yet, with dementia, the patient isn't the only casualty.'

'Aw, Mom! Don't start!'

Hearing both pain and impatience in Michael's voice, Dee slipped down the steps and returned to the truck to wait.

Michael wasn't long in joining her. He'd changed into casual wear too. Nothing in his manner betrayed the emotion of the conversation she'd overheard. Giving him high marks for compartmentalizing his life, Dee gave him his space and didn't mention his grandfather.

There was a mob at Trevor's, just as Michael'd predicted. Dee had forgotten, until she spotted Tulip Johnson, that Tulip's mother was married to Trevor's father, which made Tulip and Trevor step-siblings. Easy enough to forget. At school, Trevor avoided Tulip like a deadly virus.

Clad in cut-off shorts and an over-sized T-shirt, Tulip was doing cannon-balls off the diving boards, drenching pool-side partiers still in street clothes. Trevor looked like he could throttle her.

General socializing gave way to an organized tournament of water volleyball. Dee and Michael were on Trevor's team. Trevor'd lettered in both swimming and diving. His competitive nature brought pressure to bear. Michael seemed okay with it. But Dee's fingers turned to thumbs. She climbed out mid-tournament after blowing game point. Tulip climbed out, too, got a big slice of watermelon and fell into the chair next to Dee.

Tulip was long-limbed, with broad shoulders and strong thighs and hands that could palm a basketball. A trim-lined suit in navy or black would have been more becoming on her than a sloppy wet T-shirt and shorts. But Tulip wasn't into stylin'.

Intercepting her glance, Tulip wiped juice from her chin with the back of her arm. 'Who was the old guy at graduation?'

Warily, Dee said, 'Michael's grandfather. Why?'

'He was sweet, that's all.' Tulip spat a seed toward a plastic pelican decorating the fence. It bounced off the bird's beak. But the second one stuck. 'Bull's eye! Go get you a slice of melon and we'll have a seed-spitting contest.'

Deanna politely declined.

Tulip launched another seed. 'Right in the gullet! Two points!' she crowed.

Relieved to see the bathroom door on the pool house swing open, Dee made for it and changed back into her sundress. When she came back out, Tulip was astride the diving board boisterously calling a play-by-play of the volleyball match.

Deanna settled into a lawn chair off the beaten path while Michael finished another game. They said their thank-yous to host and hostess, and drove to Sally's house half a mile out of town.

Sally's dad was a long-haul trucker with a fondness for fireworks. Kids crowded into the backyard on lawn chairs and blankets and in the dewy grass for his display. Dee and Michael settled on beach towels just as Mr Simmons put the first match to fuse. Starbursts of red, yellow and green soared heavenward in rapid succession. Laughing, Dee joined a group count. 'Sixteen, seventeen, eighteen, nineteen, twenty.'

Spontaneous applause erupted as the twenty-first starburst faded into puffs of drifting smoke. That was just the beginning. Sally's dad set off a non-stop display for the next forty minutes. When it was finished, some of the kids drifted back toward the patio and the house beyond. But Michael seemed in no hurry. Stretching out on his back, hands locked behind his head, he mused, 'Fireworks and neon. Now there's a thought.'

'Like a laser light show?'

'Sort of, but not exactly. It's something to think about.'

Deanna hugged her knees to her chest and smiled down at him. 'Mick, the neon man. Gonna light up the night.'

'It's more than light, it's an art form. And it's catching on again. Trick is to figure out how to make it work for you.'

'As a career?'

He nodded. Dee didn't know much about neon. She did know Michael was a natural mechanic and a pretty fair electrician. He'd been fixing things at their house for years. 'Do you go to school for neon?' she asked.

'You can,' he said. 'But it's pretty expensive. I've been reading up on it, and I think, with the right equipment, I can teach myself to bend glass.'

'For real?'

'Sure. Why not? I'm thinking about Grandpa's

shop on Grove Street. It'd be a good location. I'll have to come up with some cash for equipment and supplies, then ease into it, learn as I go.'

'Sounds like a plan to me.'

Michael grinned and reached up to tug at her ponytail. 'Want to share space? You can have your toppings shop out in front. I'll even make you a sign: "Dee's Toppings – No Nude Food Served".'

'Or nude customers.' Dee laughed.

'What's so funny?' Sally came their way with a tray of cold sodas.

'We're talking career opportunities.' Dee reached for a soda. 'Thanks, Sally. Super party.'

'The fireworks are great.' Michael chimed in.

'Dad's contribution.'

Dee cooled her dry throat and took mental notes. Next year, when she graduated, she wanted a party just like this. *Her* dad wasn't much for catering to kids, though. She thought fleetingly of Pru writing in her diary, *'Father is so burdened by the journey, he makes laughter look like work.'* Dad was kind of like that, too, so caught up in making a living, he forgot how to have fun. She tugged at Sally and asked, 'How'd you get such a cool dad?'

'Are you kidding? He's the biggest kid here.'

'Runs in the family.' Chisel Parker sauntered over, the sharp angles of his face shaping a careless grin.

'You're ate up, Chisel. Make like a drum and beat it,' Sally feigned boredom in this unsolicited attention from the best drummer in the school band.

Chisel hummed a few bars in harmony with the CD that was playing and tapped out the beat on Sally's shoulder. Sally giggled and swatted Chisel's hand away. He caught her arm, pulled it behind her back and pretended he was going to twist it. Courtship, Chisel style.

Dee got to her feet, intending to answer nature's call. But Michael rose beside her.

'It's good music. You want to dance?'

She looked toward the house and saw couples gathering on the lighted deck. 'Sounds good. But I gotta visit the little girls' room first, okay?'

'Be right back.'

'Wait up, Dee. I'm coming, too,' said Sally.

Deanna turned, waiting for Sally to catch up with her.

Chisel called, 'Dee! That reminds me. The old guy sitting next to you at graduation? Who is he, anyway?'

Deanna's gaze flew to meet Chisel's, fearful of what was about to come out of his mouth. *He'd played in the band. He'd seen Mr Kolupa dance! His whole evening of antics.* In the same split-second frame, she saw the blood drain from Michael's face. Her heart froze as she willed Chisel to swallow his words. *Walk on. Walk on and ignore him and maybe he'll shut up.* Her legs were brittle, lifeless sticks. Slow. Clumsy. Too ponderous to outdistance Chisel's boom box voice.

'He stole a flag from the park today. I plastered him with a water balloon. You should have heard the old geezer squeal!'

Dee cringed at the sound of his laughter, every muscle tensed. Afraid to turn. Two seconds, three. Listening with a fatal certainty for the sound of damaging fury and flying, flesh-bruising fists. Four seconds, five.

'What's with him?'

It was Chisel's voice, puzzled, seeking.

Dee turned to see Michael crossing the yard toward the grassy field of parked vehicles. Shoulders bunched. Hands clenched. Long, angry, ground-eating strides. Heart twisting, she started after him. She wondered, as she drew even with Chisel, how *anyone* could plaster an old man with a water balloon.

Intercepting her black scowl, Chisel yelped, 'What'd *I* do? All I said was. . .'

'That was Michael's grandfather, you jerk!' Dee hissed.

Chisel's jaw dropped as she shoved past.

'Be fair, Dee. He didn't know,' protested Sally in a conciliatory tone.

Dee kept walking. She slipped silently into the truck where Michael was waiting. He turned the key and switched on the lights without saying a word. Her pulse throbbed in an aching throat. She stole a sidelong glance. 'You want to talk about it?'

'What's to say?'

There was an edge to his voice. She'd heard it before. When Dad'd had a bad day and Mom was trying with the best of intentions to put things in their proper perspective. Is that what it took to be a woman? Soothing words? If so, she was a failure. She had no words. And too little courage. She didn't know how to draw Michael out when he clearly wanted to be left alone.

It was a silent ride home. Dee's eye was drawn to the neon light in the McKinsey's front window. It seemed in its glaring gaiety to mock their misery.

Michael walked her to the door, elbows bent, fingertips in his pockets. Even his eyebrows looked tense.

'Forget Chisel,' she urged quietly. 'He's got drumsticks for brains.'

'It isn't just Chisel.' Behind the anger was pain.

Dee moved closer. Slipped one arm around his waist in a tentative hug. But he held himself rigid, refusing to yield to comfort. The impulse of kindness turned awkward. Her arm fell away as he stepped back.

'I'm sorry, Dee. I shouldn't have. . .' Michael rocked back on his heels, bit his lip and sighed again. 'This isn't going to work. Things are just too. . .' He paused, struggling for words, then gave up the search and backed off the porch. The moon-gilded grass cushioned his steps. Half-way across the yard, he called back, 'Forget I said it was a date, okay?'

Earlier, she'd been having such a good time, she *had* forgotten. And yet, somehow, the reminder stung. Dee lifted her chin, shrugged, and forced a smile. 'Whatever.'

'You're not mad?'

'Course not.'

'You're sure?'

'Thanks for the lift, Michael. See you.' Dee's pony-tail swished across her face as she turned and fumbled for the door. Her heart was pounding, her palms clammy. *Why was she feeling shaken and all-aflush? It was just Michael, not some drop-dead gorgeous date of a lifetime!* Reminded of Pru's first entry concerning Seth Hickman, Dee tiptoed to her room, commiserating with Pru's puzzled, *'His eyes are a fetching shade of blue. But he's too lean and too gangly and he murders the English language in that backwoods way of his. So why did my heart catch when he returned to camp with our lost cow in tow?'*

Why, indeed?

Chapter 5

'*Turn the other cheek? I should have slugged the guy. Dropped him where he stood. What's the matter with me? He called Grandpa an old geezer. Hit him with a water balloon. My* grandfather.'

Michael lifted his hands from the keyboard and rubbed stinging eyes. There was enough rage left, he could find Chisel, settle the score. But he wouldn't. Not because he'd learned to fight with wits instead of fists. And not because he feared getting hurt. The anguish inside was worse than punishing blows. He was ashamed. Embarrassed. Afraid what people would think. What Dee would think. He forced himself to put it in black and white.

'*Ashamed. Embarrassed. Afraid.*'

His finger hovered over the delete key. But he let the words stand. It was true. Mom said he didn't need to be, but he was. Grandpa's strange behavior, his lost words, his befuddled look strained his patience at home. But when he was in public, and people were stealing glances or out and out staring, it was excruciating.

Was it just the flag thing? Or had Grandpa done

something at graduation to catch Chisel's eye?
Michael's thoughts squirmed from beneath the glare of painful self-examination. Mom said things had gone smoothly. But her gaze slid away as she said it. He'd wanted to believe her. Dee was waiting and he'd been eager to be with her, though he'd managed, before the evening was over, to screw that up too. He should have skipped graduation. Or talked Mom out of taking Grandpa with her when Aunt Sheri couldn't come. *Did he dance? Feed the birds? Talk to the chairs?*

He doesn't deserve to be like this. It isn't fair.

The blinking cursor melted into the angry blur of words. Michael pushed back his chair and turned off the ceiling light. His computer screen reflected the neon sign in his window. Something about it wasn't right. He turned and saw the 'c' wasn't lighted. The gas had escaped, extinguishing that one letter. He gazed at the sign, thinking of Grandpa, losing it a letter at a time. Chest tight, he kicked off his shoes, stretched out on the bed and railed against such senseless seepage.

Take care of Grandpa. Piece of cake, he'd thought. Such a noble hot-shot. Now look at him. A week and he wanted to blame fate, blame God, blame Mom, blame Chisel, blame anyone who played any part in this burning knot in his throat. The phone rang. Thinking of Dee, Michael stretched a hand toward the nightstand, heart knocking. But it was Uncle Walt. The baby was a boy. Seven pounds, nine ounces. Twenty-one inches.

'Bald as a door-knob, but healthy and whole. We're glad it's over,' said Walt. 'Sheri did just great.'

'Have you chosen a name?'

'Looks like we're going to go with Ira Earl.'

'After Grandpa Kolupa?'

'That's right. What do you think? Will your Grandpa like that?'

'Sure,' said Michael. *If you can make him understand.*

Mom picked up the extension, and asked in a sleepy voice, 'Walt? I thought that'd be you. How's Sheri?'

Leaving his uncle to repeat it all, Michael hung up, turned off his computer, shed his clothes and crawled between the sheets.

Mom poked her head in the door a few moments later. Silhouetted by the wall light, she asked him about the parties and Dee and did he have fun? He didn't tell her how things had gone from good to bad to worse. Or pin her down on what Grandpa had or hadn't done at graduation. He told her instead about Trevor's pool and Sally's dad's fireworks display. And that, in the morning, he was taking Grandpa down to the shop on Grove Street. They'd sew the flag and take it back to the park.

'Dad'll enjoy that.' She yawned widely, then hurried away, head cocked.

Michael heard it too – Grandpa's door creaking on its hinges.

61

'Who is that? Who's there?' Grandpa called, a wary note in his voice.

Michael started to get up. 'He's not so hot for sleeping.'

'Stay where you are. The night shift is mine.' Leaving his door ajar, his mother padded down the hallway, calling softly to Grandpa so as not to startle him.

Michael lay back on his pillow. He wanted to pull the covers over his head. To forget for a while the day behind and the summer ahead and Dee next door, adding to his misery. It was a catch-22. Wanting to be closer, and at the same time knowing a deeper relationship meant being open with her about Grandpa. Even if he could be that honest, which he doubted, she was probably fed up by now.

Out in the hall, Mom was trying to coax Grandpa into returning to his room. 'It's after midnight, Dad. You should be in bed.'

'I can't. There's a lady looking ... locking ... lolling. She's lolling on my bed,' said Grandpa.

'A lady? Dad, you're mistaken. There's no one here but you and me and Michael.'

'What?'

'The doors are locked. How could she get in?' Mom reasoned.

'What?'

'There is no woman on your bed, Dad.' Mom tried in the same modulated tone to calm Grandpa's paranoia, for it wasn't his hearing, rather his comprehension that made him ask, 'What?'

But Grandpa clung stubbornly to the notion. 'There's a lady. I'd go to bed, but she's lolling on it.'

'Come out to the kitchen. I'll fix a nice cup of cocoa,' Mom tried to distract him.

Michael lay listening to their voices retreat. She would tell him about the baby. Little Ira Earl. Come too late to know the wonderful grandfather Michael had known. Too late for piggyback rides. For treadle machines and little league games and paraphrased proverbs, like: 'Even a fool, when he keeps his mouth shut, is considered wise.'

He should have kept his mouth shut. Let them send him to the home. He wouldn't be in this fix. Disliking himself for being so spineless, Michael longed for the old days when Grandpa could quote Scripture without moving chairs. He sighed, put tired feet on the floor and pulled on his sweats. Could he retrieve a scrap of what was lost? Acting on a hunch, he grabbed his truck keys and the flag and trekked out to the kitchen.

Mom turned from a rattling search for the cocoa pan and eyed him in surprise. 'Are you going some-where?'

'To the shop. You can go back to bed. I'm taking him with me.'

'Who, Dad?' The worn-out lines of Mom's pudgy face puckered into a frown. 'It's the middle of the night. He isn't even dressed.'

'That didn't stop him this morning.' Michael

stopped in front of Grandpa's chair. He touched one blue-veined hand. 'Do you want to go for a ride, Grandpa?'

'There's a woman lurking.' Grandpa's wrinkles and lines drooped into a petulant frown. 'She's lulling. . .lolling on my bed.'

Mom nudged him, a tired twinkle in her eye. 'Accept it, Michael. She's lolling.'

Another time, he might have grinned. But not tonight. Nothing would help, not even comic relief. He stretched an arm across his grandfather's shoulder. 'Let her loll, Grandpa. Let's you and me go downtown.'

Mom looked like she thought there was an epidemic of lost reason. But she quit objecting, got Grandpa his hat and a robe to wear over his pajamas and walked them both out to the truck.

'Where's Stella?' asked Grandpa as Michael helped him in. 'Isn't she coming?'

Stella was Michael's grandmother. Reluctant to remind Grandpa of that distant loss, Michael said, 'She couldn't come. She was busy. Hold the flag, would you, Grandpa?'

The distraction worked. Grandpa unfolded the flag, then spent the short ride trying to keep it up off the floor. Street lights shone down on a deserted business district. Grandpa's brick shop was squeezed between a shoe store and a movie theater, an old relic the history buffs were trying to raise funds to restore.

Grandpa's name was lettered in gold leaf on the

darkened shop window. Aunt Sheri had posted a *Furnished Apartment for Rent* sign on the door.

'Thank you for the ride,' Grandpa reached for the door handle as Michael cut the headlights.

'Wait a second, I'm coming in too.'

'It's late. I'm going to bed,' said Grandpa.

Michael knew instinctively it wouldn't be a good idea to let him go upstairs. Mom and Aunt Sheri, hoping to defray the expenses of upkeep and taxes through rental income, had cleared out Grandpa's personal possessions from the apartment, leaving only a few pieces of furniture. It was only because of Michael's interest in establishing a shop from which he could make and sell neon signs that they hadn't cleared out the downstairs to rent, too. Michael circled the truck and opened the passenger door.

The ring of keys swinging from his index finger caught Grandpa's eye. He patted his pockets, the forgotten flag slipping to the floor of the truck. 'Where. . .have I lost my keys?'

'Never mind, Grandpa. I'll unlock it.' Michael grabbed the flag and folded it under his arm.

'Keep it off the. . .off the. . .out of the dirt,' said Grandpa. He waved a knotty finger toward the flag. 'There's rules about those. . .'

'Flags?'

'No,' said Grandpa. But he nodded.

Mental fatigue was taking a toll on his vocabulary. But he didn't seem physically tired. He ignored Michael's arm, stepped on to the curb unassisted, lumbered to the door of the shop and put his face to the glass. Michael gently nudged him aside and unlocked the door.

Grandpa pushed right past him. His hand reached unerringly for the switch, bathing the shop in light. He took off his hat, his robe too, and hung them from wooden pegs near the door. For a moment he stood motionless, eyes wide open, breathing deeply as if drawing strength from this shop where he'd spent the past half century. He wandered the length of the front room. The wooden floor echoed his steps. His fingers trailed along the window-sill. He brushed a dusty cobweb from the corner. Circled the scarred counter. Turned the crank on the old cash register where he'd rung up countless tabs for customers. Michael jumped at the sound of the bell. His heart hammered hope. He seemed less vacant. More. . .with it. Could there be healing in this place?

'Dusty,' said Grandpa. He wiped his finger on his pajama leg, then reached beneath the counter for the sweeping compound. 'They'll be here soon.'

With no clue to the path his thoughts had taken, Michael took the flag into the back room. He returned with the broom and began sweeping. Grandpa took it from him.

'You get the. . .what is it? Not benches.' He waved his hand impatiently. 'Chairs, get the chairs.'

That, again? What was it with the chairs?

Holding out for a secret door, a way of breaking through, Michael tried again. 'I'm going to trim back this flag. You want to help?'

Grandpa didn't even look up, just kept scattering the sweeping compound with the broom.

Michael walked on back to the workroom alone. Leaving the door open so he could hear Grandpa moving about, he spread the flag on the table. He found a yardstick, marked a straight line, then cut away the ravelings made by the wind.

'Grandpa? You want to come help? he called from the door.

Grandpa brought the broom with him. He looked on as Michael turned the edge up twice, but made no effort to help pin the hem in place. Michael sat down at the machine.

'Change the thread,' said Grandpa.

Encouraged by the moment of clarity, Michael moved out of the way. 'You change it.'

Grandpa sat down at the machine. And sat. And looked. And touched. Fidgeting fingers began to poke and prod and push and pull at the tension gauge, the thread guide, the bobbin release. He looked up in irritation when the bobbin popped out.

'I told her to have that. . .that. . .that. . .'

'Bobbin?'

'Yes. I told her to have it fixed.' He got out of the chair, and beckoned toward an empty rack. 'All that work. Where is she, anyway?'

Knowing he meant Grandma, Michael's hope

67

shriveled like a dried grape. He swallowed his disappointment and said, 'She's okay. Grandpa. Don't worry.'

'Did she go. . .' Growing more agitated, Grandpa paced to the door and looked out on to the front room. 'Did she go. . .' He shuffled his feet.

'Dancing? No, Grandpa. Of course not.'

'She does, you know. She loves to dance. But not with me. We never go dancing any more.'

'She can't Grandpa.'

'She never goes with me. We never go. . .' His voice trailed off.

Michael put an arm around his shoulder and felt it tremble. A throbbing at the base of his neck swept up, spread out, dulling his thoughts. This was a dumb idea. They shouldn't have come.

'I'm tired, Grandpa. You want to go home? Let's go home. We can come another time and finish the flag, okay?'

Grandpa said, 'No.' But he said it without conviction, and didn't resist being led into the front room. They were almost to the front door when a face appeared at the window. Michael's nerves jumped. Instinctively, he pressed closer to Grandpa as knuckles rapped against glass.

'Mr Kolupa? Is there a problem?' an unfamiliar voice called.

The hat and the uniform were that of a city cop. Michael unlocked the door, identified himself and explained they'd come to mend a flag.

Middle-aged and too well seasoned to betray his thoughts by expression, the officer must have had his doubts about Michael. He asked for ID. Michael admitted he'd come away without any.

The policeman looked from Michael to Grandpa. 'Are you all right, sir?'

Grandpa stared at the badge on the man's uniform. 'No.'

'He just says that,' Michael hastened to explain as the cop's attention shifted back to him. 'He's been sick.'

Expression unchanged, the officer asked, 'Mind if I take a look in the back room?'

'No. Go ahead.'

The officer wasn't gone long. The flag draped over the machine must have convinced him. There was an apology in his tone as he explained, 'There's been no activity around here for the last couple of weeks. When I saw the lights, I thought I'd better check on Mr Kolupa. Hope I didn't alarm you.'

'No. We were just leaving anyway,' said Michael.

'Lock her up tight, then.' The officer was almost out of the door when he turned back. 'By the way, Mr Kolupa. You haven't been around to the Police Department in a long time. We've had to throw our flags away and get new ones. Be a lot cheaper to keep them sewed.'

'Maybe we'll be by,' said Michael.

The officer tipped his hat and turned away again.

Grandpa asked as the door closed behind him,

'Are we going to. . .to. . .to. . .you know, where they lock you up?'

'No, Grandpa,' said Michael, helping him into his robe. 'He was checking about the lights, that's all.'

'What?'

'He saw the lights.'

'What?'

'We aren't going to gaol.'

Grandpa accepted his hat from Michael with an unsteady hand. 'They tell me it isn't gaol. But the doors are locked.'

'You aren't in gaol, Grandpa,' Michael tried to reassure him.

Grandpa wagged his head and quietly mused, 'That's what they say. But I don't know.'

Had his world narrowed to where it felt like a cell? Michael's eyes stung. But he got the door for him, assuring, 'You aren't in gaol. Honest, Grandpa. You aren't."

Chapter 6

'Haven't heard a word from Truckers' Plaza, but it's only been a few days. Michael wrote me a thank-you note. It was polite and impersonal. I see him out in the yard, looking on as his grandpa messes with the lawn chairs or giving him bread crusts for the birds. (Sometimes, Mr Kolupa forgets and eats them.) If Michael sees me and lifts his hand, I lift mine. But I haven't been over there and he hasn't been over here. No doubt about it, graduation night ended in a fizzle.'

Dee opened her bedroom curtains to see Mr Kolupa out on the deck addressing the lawn chairs. His long-sleeved shirt was buttoned from the collar down and tucked into his trousers. His suspenders were snapped into place, but he was hatless. Perspiration beaded his bald head. His lips moved, his hands fluttered to his sides like leaves in a listless breeze.

Alice came in from the bathroom, a towel draped around her wet hair. 'What are you looking at?'

'Nothing.'

Alice slipped up beside her. Smelling of tooth-paste and fingernail polish, she struck a pose so like Mr Kolupa, it was uncanny. Fingers spread, gently fluttering, she said in a dry whisper, "'O wretched man that I am! Who shall deliver me from the body of death?'"

'Cut it out, Alice,' said Dee, though it was hard not to snicker at her sister's expert mimicry.

Alice flashed her flawless white smile. 'That's what he's saying. Over and over. Watch his lips. I don't know how Michael stands it.'

'Like you're such a picnic.' Dee moved away from the window. Brown petals still floated in the rose-bowl on her dresser. The ribbon, the florist's tape and the pearl pin that had held the corsage together lay on the bottom in cloudy water.

Alice made a face. 'Why don't you throw that disgusting thing out?'

'Doug's watching to see if it will grow. I told him it wouldn't, but I guess he wants to see for himself.'

'What a dweeb.'

Dee wondered why Alice could never see the sweetness in Doug. She asked, 'Isn't Mom expecting you at the shop?'

'Some job. I'm just a gofer.'

'She's got a broken foot, what do you expect?'

'I could work the register. It'd be more interesting than dusting all that old junk she's collected. And hammering and gluing and fixing what's broken.'

'Doug's a born fixer-upper. Mom should have

72

hired him instead of you.'

'Don't I wish! I'm not even there yet, and I'm bored.'

'You're not bored, you're boring.'

'You're such a grouch!' Alice complained. 'Like it's my fault Michael's avoiding you.'

'Who said he was avoiding me?' Dee managed not to flinch.

Alice smirked. 'He takes you out once, and for the next five days hides away in the house.'

'He didn't take me out. It was a lift, that's all.'

'What'd you do to him, anyway?' Alice ignored the denial.

The ringing phone spared Dee a response. Alice the Meddling Critic lunged for it.

'Yolanda! I was on my way to call you. Just a second, I'm going to change phones.'

Immune to Dee's provoked glance, Alice turned away and dashed out the door. She was a pain. Aggravating. Exasperating. Irritating. None of Pru's younger sisters could have been as big a pain.

'I've got it, Dee. Hang it up, okay?' the troll called from the living-room.

Dee returned the phone to the receiver and crossed back to the window. Mr Kolupa was still there. She could slip out on the pretense of cutting a bouquet of lilacs. Stage a 'chance encounter' when Michael came out to urge his grandfather inside out of the hot-eyed sun. Pretend she'd dismissed graduation night. Or bring it up and clear the air, once and for all. But she wouldn't, and she couldn't even say why. Except that it was awkward.

Doug came around the side of the house, push-ing his bicycle. Band-aids criss-crossed both knees. Dee watched through the window as he leaned the bike against the towering red maple in the yard, glanced toward Michael's back yard, then backed away. In less than a ten-count, he called to her from the front door.

'Dee? Help me ride my bike, okay?'

'It's too hot, Doug. Maybe later.'

'It's not too hot. I want to ride now. *Please?*'

Dee suspected he didn't want her help so much as someone to protect him from Mr Kolupa. She'd told him and told him Mr Kolupa didn't have a dungeon and that he wasn't going to hurt him or anyone else. But Doug took the same 'anything's possible' stance he'd taken with the disintegrated corsage. Except his attitude toward long-dead flowers was guardedly optimistic, while his attitude toward Mr Kolupa was all negative. Alice had worked her mischief well. Doug kept pleading until finally she sighed and caved in, promising, 'I'll be out in a little bit.'

'Dee?' Alice called from the living-room. 'Sally wants you. Make it quick. I've got to call Mom and tell her I'm going to be a little late.'

Dee hadn't talked to Sally since the day after Carl's party. The subject of Michael's abrupt leave-taking had come up. Things had gotten a little tense when Dee defended Michael's anger with Chisel. Sally maintained Chisel'd meant no harm,

74

that he simply hadn't realized the connection.

Dee picked up the phone. 'You can hang up, Alice.'

'Thought Alice was running the shop with your mom,' said Sally after the click.

'The only thing she's running is her mouth and a dustcloth.'

Sally chuckled. 'How's the babysitting going?'

Relieved all traces of strain had evaporated between them, Dee said, 'I took the training wheels off Doug's bike yesterday.'

'Master the two-wheeler, has he?'

'He's got a system for the starts. It's the stops that are peeling the skin off his knees.' Lapping the cord around her finger, Dee asked, 'What've you been up to?'

'Went to the movies with Chisel last night. You were right about him. He *is* an insensitive jerk.'

Dee played it safe and ventured in a neutral voice, 'Anything good playing?'

'How would I know? Chisel was so busy being a one-man entertainment committee, I didn't hear half of it,' complained Sally.

'Maybe he should ask Tulip out.'

'I wouldn't wish him on Tulip. She, at least, is unique. Chisel, on the other hand, is a bore.' Sally hesitated for a second, then asked, 'Any interesting mail?'

Dee made the leap from male to mail. 'No.'

'Phone calls? Post-its?'

'Huh-uh. Why? Should there be?'

'It's just that. . .that is. . .I may as well tell you. Truckers' Plaza called. I'm supposed to go in at two.'

'You're hired?'

'Looks that way.'

'Lucky dog!' cried Dee, shot through with envy.

'The diner last summer was mostly coffee drinkers. But this is fast-paced. Hope I can keep up.'

'You'll do fine,' Dee said quickly. 'And who knows? Maybe they'll call me, too.'

'That's what I'm hoping. I'll put in a plug, okay?'

'Thanks, Sally. That'd be great.'

'You want to go to the mall? Do some shopping, grab a bite of lunch?'

'It's tempting, but I better not. Doug's not much for shopping,' said Dee after a moment's hesitation. 'Besides, I want to be here if Truckers' Plaza calls.'

'Sure. I understand.'

'Dee? I thought you were coming out?' Doug hollered from the front door.

'I've gotta go. But be sure and call me tonight,' Dee told Sally. 'I want to hear all about your first day.'

'It'll be kind of late when I get off. I'll wait until morning to call.'

'Just as well. Dad growls if the phone rings after ten.'

'Tell me about it!' said Sally.

Dee chuckled as she hung up the phone. Dad

was a grouch, sometimes. Mom said he worked too hard. Maybe that was just the way of men, for Pru, in her diary, had commented upon her father's temperament in an entry made just a few days out of Independence, Missouri. She reached for the diary and read:

'*We crossed the Vermillion River today. It wasn't a bit deep, nor large like the Kansas River, but it lay at the bottom of a steep-walled canyon. Each wagon had to be lowered by ropes to the river bottom, then hauled up the other side. The live-stock had to be taken across in the same manner. It was dark by the time we made camp. Father was so tired, he fell asleep with his plate in his lap. At the sound of our giggles, he jerked awake, then scolded us soundly for being rowdy. Mother hushed our protests, and before the clean-up was half-started, Father was asleep again.*'

'Dee?' Doug wailed again.

'I'm coming!' Dee closed the diary and hurried out to keep Doug safe from poor old harmless Mr Kolupa.

Michael's corner bedroom had two windows, one facing Dee's house, the other the backyard. Both were wide open, even though the only breeze coming through was a hot one. After Grandpa's comment about gaol, he'd felt guilty over the gate he'd stretched across the steps leading from the deck into the yard. But short of staying by his side, he knew of no other way to keep him from wandering off. He could hear him reciting the same

Scripture verse over and over again, his once-strong voice blending into the background of birds twitting and stirring leaves and a cricket under the window.

Michael crossed to his computer and sat down. He had a pretty good idea what he needed in a neon room, and money might soon be less of a problem. The cop the other night had given him an idea about how he could begin funding the project. But he didn't have much building experience, and there was a wall in his way. Was it safe to knock it out? Or was it a load-bearing wall that shouldn't be removed? And what about safety codes and fire codes and building permits?

He know too little about these things that would have been second nature to Grandpa a few years ago. Now with Grandpa's volumes of knowledge slowly leaking away, it struck him that they were on opposite ends of learning. Thoughts shifting, Michael loaded a program on floor plans, intending to turn the rough sketch he'd made on the back of an envelope into something concrete and precise. But the program, with its numbers and choices, raised more questions than it answered.

Discouraged and easily distracted, he listened to Doug next door nagging at Dee to come outside. If she answered, he didn't hear her. He strained his ear, listening for Grandpa.

'"O wretched man that I am, who shall deliver me from this body of death."' It came to him as if from a great distance. Feeling wretched himself,

Michael mopped the sweat from his face and wished he could turn on the air. But he'd have to close up the house first. And if he closed up the house, he couldn't hear Grandpa.

'Ride to the sidewalk,' Dee's voice drew him to the open window.

Band-aids on both knees, Doug ran to the red maple where his bicycle was parked. 'See, Dee. I can start it by myself!'

Michael watched as Doug, with Dee looking on, leaned the bike against the tree. He straddled the seat and pushed off from the tree. The bike wobbled to the left, to the right, to the left. The front tire hit a shallow dip in the lawn.

'Hang on!' cried Dee. But the bike went down.

Doug lay there a moment, wincing and rubbing his shin.

'You're okay.' Dee helped Doug up, then wheeled the bike back to the tree. 'Try it again.'

Teetering on the seat, Doug looked to make sure she was watching.

'Got your balance? Go ahead!' she urged.

Doug gripped the handlebars. He eased his foot off the left pedal, pushed away and weaved a shaky path toward the walk.

'Good job! See? You can do it! You don't need me!' said Dee, staying between him and the street.

Doug turned down the walk and kept pedalling. Michael couldn't see him for the houses. Dee took off after him. In seconds, he couldn't see her either. But he could hear her calling, 'Stop at the corner, Doug. Don't ride into the street!'

As he stood listening, the scene brought back memories of his father coming out on to the porch one morning with a wrench in his hand. 'A big fella like you should have been riding without these a long time ago,' he'd said. Michael remembered the knot in his stomach as he'd watched Dad take off those training wheels. With each fall, he'd felt more dismal, fearing Dad's impatience, his disappointment, until finally, Dad gave up and Mom came out. Though Dad was probably the better rider, Mom, with her confidence in his capabilities, soon had him riding.

It was a simple truth. But it translated well. He was, by his self-doubts, defeating himself on this neon room thing before he'd ever got started. Realizing as much, Michael decided to try it again later when there were fewer distractions. Right now, Grandpa could probably use a cold drink and some company.

Michael closed up the house, turned on the air and fixed two glasses of iced water before sliding the deck door open. His heart kicked to his throat. The chairs were all empty. The gate hung open. He'd been wrong in assuming Grandpa couldn't open it. *He was nowhere to be seen.*

'Grandpa?' Michael vaulted down the steps, raced across the yard, looked up and down the graveled alley. The front yard was just as empty. He ran into the street, and looked both ways, calling as he went. Dee would help him. But there was no sign of her either. Forcing back panic, he ran in the same direction Doug had headed on his rocky ride down the walk.

Michael turned the corner and saw Dee racing up the walk ahead of him. A dozen yards further on were Grandpa, Doug, and Doug's bicycle, the back wheel still spinning. Deliberately, he slowed his steps and swallowed the scolding words that chased on the heels of relief as Grandpa stooped over and tried to help Doug to his feet.

Doug, on his back with the bike on top of him, strained away from Grandpa. 'Dee! Help!'

Concerned he was hurt, Michael broke into a run. He reached Doug just seconds behind Dee to find Grandpa tugging at the chain of keys that dangled from Doug's belt loop. Seeing the Singer medallion clipped to the ring, understanding came swiftly. But Dee was in his way.

'Let go, Mr Kolupa!' she said, dropping to her knees to intervene.

'Help me!' Doug's voice broke as he wriggled sideways, trying to free himself from the bike and from Grandpa's grip on his key-chain.

'Calm down, Doug. You're scaring him,' Michael warned.

Dee whirled around, surprise turning to indignation. 'Scaring *him?* It's Doug who. . . Do something, Michael!'

'Easy, Doug,' Michael reached down, placed his hands over Grandpa's and said quietly, 'It's okay, Grandpa. You can let go. I'll get them.'

Sweat streamed down the seams of Grandpa's face, 'No, no, no!' He tugged all the harder.

Dee's name came out a strangled sob as Doug rooted his heels into the grass, trying to break free.

Michael said in the same level voice, 'The keys were his, Doug. He wants them back. I'll get you another set, okay?'

Doug's chin wobbled, but he stopped struggling and let Michael unclip the keys and give them to Grandpa. He closed his hand around the medallion, straightened and backed away.

'You took them. That's a bad boy.' Grandpa shook a gnarled finger at Doug.

'Huh-uh,' Doug sniffed. On his feet, clinging to Dee, he tipped his face and whispered, 'Tell him, Dee.'

Cheeks flushed, Dee addressed Michael instead. 'They were in a box of cast-offs. Your mom said Doug could have them.'

'Guess she didn't realize Grandpa'd be sentimental about them.'

Temper flared in her eyes. 'He got a watch out of the same box. Suppose you want that back, too.'

Doug yelped a protest.

'No, not unless. . .' Ears hot, Michael shifted his gaze to Doug. Lowering his voice, he said, 'Just keep it in your pocket, okay?'

Doug nodded, looking relieved. But Dee sniffed, jerked his bike up off the ground and said, 'Come on, Doug. Climb on.'

Michael stood, arm around Grandpa, wanting to

explain that Grandpa didn't remember that most of his things had been sold or given away. But he couldn't talk about him with him standing right there. So he sucked it in, and stood silently by as Dee, chin leading the way, strode after Doug and his weaving bike.

Chapter 7

'Georgia leaves for camp on Sunday. I'm going to miss her, especially with Sally working so many hours. Speaking of Sally, she called this morning. Guess she's making pretty good tips at the Plaza. (That's what she calls it – the Plaza.) I'm disappointed they haven't called me to work. But hey! Disappointment is my life!'

Thunder rumbled like a distant freight train. It's been trying to rain all day, but so far without success. Alice was at the shop with their mother and Doug was in the bathroom. Dee hadn't checked, but she thought he was washing the rocks he'd collected yesterday on their way to Memorial Park. The flag Mr Kolupa had snatched was flying again. Or perhaps it was a new one, she had no way of knowing.

'I was over at Georgia's house last night when Michael brought a set of keys for Doug. The key-chain is retractable, like the vacuum cleaner cord. Fancy, smancy. Doug is more scared than ever of Mr Kolupa. But, thanks to the key-chain, Michael's getting high marks with the kid. Mom caught the

*drift that all is not well between Michael and I. She
says I should be sensitive, that it can't be any picnic taking care of a man whose mind and feet both
wander. I tried to tell her MICHAEL'S avoiding
ME! He stays inside with his grandpa all day, then
takes off the minute his mom gets home from work
and doesn't return until ten, eleven, even midnight.
I bet he's seeing that Cheryl person again.'*

Dee ate the last wedge of apple spread in crunchy
peanut butter, raisins and M & M's. She licked her
fingers, then kicked off her shoes and stretched out
on her bed to reread what she'd written. That last
line sounded sour. Maybe she *was* sour. And not
over the key thing, either. Though she hadn't admitted it out loud, she could see how Michael may have
known no other way of handling it. And, according
to Doug, he *did* say he was sorry when he came over
last night. His avoiding her, that's what hurt. Up to
a point, she'd had a really good time graduation
night. She'd even got a stomach flutter when he'd
thrown her that rose. And again later, when he'd
asked her to dance. Then Chisel flapped his big jaws
and ruined the evening. Still, that wasn't *her* fault. A
dozen times or more, she'd thought about going to
Michael and talking things out. But what if she
went, and he brushed her off?

The phone rang, a welcome diversion. It was
Georgia. She wanted to get together one last time
before she left for camp. Dee dodged Alice's magazines, dirty clothes and soda cans on her way to
the window-seat. She curled up with the phone

balanced on her knees. 'You want to go to Truckers' Plaza for Cokes?'

'The Plaza?'

'We'll surprise Sally. It'll be fun. You don't care if Doug comes, do you?'

'Doug's welcome. But how about that little tea room downtown instead?' Georgia suggested.

'I want to see Sally in action, don't you?'

'Guess I'm okay with it if you are,' Georgia relented.

Knowing she was being sensitive to her 'rejected' status, Dee said, 'I'm happy Sally's got a job where she's making good money. *Really*.'

'You're a good sport, Sport,' said Georgia.

Dee shrugged off the compliment and fanned her face with her journal. 'How soon are you coming?'

'Can you be ready in ten?'

'No problem.'

Dee called her plans to Doug, then changed into jeans and a cream-colored sleeveless silk shirt. It closed with pearl snaps and was fringed at the V-shaped front and back yokes. She didn't own a pair of cowboy boots. The best she could do was a pair of pointy-toed shoes reminiscent of Dorothy in *The Wizard of Oz*.

'Doug? Are you ready?' Dee knocked first, then let herself into the bathroom. Doug turned, the electric toothbrush in hand. It wasn't rocks after all, rather the rusty old key on his new key-chain he'd been washing.

87

'I used toothpaste. It does a good job. See?'
Doug held up a shiny key for her inspection.

Dee was relieved to see it wasn't *her* brush he'd
been using, rather Alice's. She held the key to the
light. 'Gleams like a Colgate smile.'

Pleased, Doug stretched out his hand, asking, as
she returned the key, 'I wonder what it goes to?'

'No way to tell, Doug. And next time? Better use
the scrub brush.' She recapped the tube of tooth-
paste and rinsed the evidence from Alice's brush.
'Let's hurry and clean this up. Georgia'll be here
any minute.'

Doug touched the fringe of her blouse. His
tongue found the space where his front teeth used
to be. 'Did you get the job? Is that why you're
wearing that shirt?'

'Not yet. But I thought I might ask about my
status. Dressing the part is a visual aid for manage-
ment.'

'Status?' echoed Doug.

'Whether they're going to hire me or not,'
explained Dee, suddenly wondering if her tactics
were a bit too transparent.

'What about me?' asked Doug.

'If I could work the same hours Sally works, I'd
still be here with you all morning and most of the
afternoon. Alice would keep you company until
Mom gets home.'

'Alice is scared of Mr Kolupa, too,' said Doug.

'Doug, he recognized his keys, that's all. You
don't have to be scared of him.' Seeing his mouth

take a stubborn line, she tried a new tactic. 'He's an antique, remember? You like antiques.'

'Just the ones we can fix,' said Doug.

The sound of a honking horn ended further discussion. Georgia was waiting. Doug had ridden with Georgia before. He got in the back and buckled his seat-belt. Dee buckled up too. Georgia braked once for kids on skateboards. But the ride to the truck stop was otherwise uneventful.

It was cool in the restaurant. Sally wore a denim apron over a long-sleeved western shirt and snug jeans that disappeared into the tops of cowboy boots. Spotting them, her thin face broke into a welcoming smile.

'What're you guys doing here?'

'Dull day. We needed a diversion,' said Georgia.

'Like watching you work,' Dee chimed in.

Sally pulled a pad of green tickets out of her apron pocket with a flourish and asked, 'So what'll it be?'

'Coke.'

'Uncola. With a big cherry, if you've got it,' added Dee.

'We don't do cola toppings, funny girl,' said Sally.

'Chocolate ice-cream cone,' said Doug.

Sally patted him on the head with her tablet. 'You buying, Dougie? Or is this on separate checks?'

'Dee's got the money,' he said.

'Spoken like every guy I've ever dated.' With

Sally-style inconsistency, she leaned her dark head closer and whispered about some guy who worked out on the drive fueling up the big rigs, and a cook who was pretty cute, too.

Dee was about to ask whom she should approach to see about her job status when she spotted a familiar figure. She tugged at Sally's apron.

'You didn't tell me Tulip Johnson worked here. When'd she start?'

'The same day I did.'

'How come you didn't mention it?'

'Guess it didn't come up.'

Dee watched Tulip climb along in her cowboy boots. The food on her tray shifted precariously as she stopped at a table across the aisle and pretended she was going to trade a squirming toddler his baby bottle for a bottle of catsup. The parents, Dee noticed, didn't look amused. 'Has she sprayed the place in perfume yet? Or spat watermelon seeds at the wall? Or belly-flopped in the jello bin?'

'Jello bin?' Sally laughed and walked away, wagging her head.

'Why don't you apply at Sunday Sundae downtown, Dee?' asked Georgia.

'She *has* a job,' Doug spoke up.

Dee smiled into his upturned face and tried not to mind that Tulip Johnson had a real job when she did not. Business was slow, but Sally couldn't sit down with them. It was against the rules. She brought their soft drinks and ice-cream, then stood visiting until she got another table of customers.

Georgia sucked the last drop from her glass and pushed it aside. 'You going to ask them about hiring you?'

They'd chosen Tulip over her – what was the use? Defeated, empty of courage Dee wagged her head. She drained her glass and gave Doug a napkin to wipe away his ice-cream smile and forced a careless tone. 'Come on, you two. Let's jet.'

On the way home, heavy clouds darkened the sky and the wind picked up. Lightning speared the western horizon with a rapid-fire strobe effect. Whorls of dust followed leaves and litter on a rough-and-tumble chase down sidewalks and alleys and into the streets.

'Listen!' Georgia cranked up the radio as she turned in Dee's driveway. It was a weather bulletin issuing a tornado warning for the Mayfield area.

Feeling uneasy, Dee tried to talk Georgia into staying. 'We're in for a downpour, by the looks of that sky. You may as well come in and wait it out.'

'I left windows open,' said Georgia. 'Mom'll snap on me if she comes home to find her oriental rug drenched.'

Dee bid her good luck at camp and promised to write. She fought the wind to the house. Dad'd given Doug a house key for his key-chain. He rushed ahead to use it. Hurrying to catch up, Dee hung on to the storm door to keep the wind from whipping it back as Doug painstakingly worked the lock.

'If Mom was here, she'd make us go to the basement. Guess that tells you what we should do,' said Dee, once they were safely inside.

'Do we have to? I don't like it down there,' Doug complained.

Surprised, Dee asked, 'Since when?'

'Alice told me about the storm shelter.'

'What *about* the storm shelter?'

Doug lowered his voice as if the walls had ears and confided. 'Alice says it was a dungeon before it was a storm shelter. There used to be rings in the wall where they chained people up.'

'Dougie, Dougie,' said Dee with a sigh. 'If that were true, we would have chained Alice up a long time ago, now wouldn't we?'

'Can't. The rings are gone,' Doug reasoned.

'There never were any rings. *That's* the story on the rings,' said Dee, but Doug remained doubtful.

Dee's attention shifted to the hail peppering the house. Her nerves tightened as the lights flickered off, then on again. She took Doug's hand and started through the house. 'Let's take a flashlight and head down just in case.'

The word 'flashlight' weakened Doug's resolve. Dad was firm about flashlights not being playthings. This, at least, was a valid reason for climbing on a chair and getting one out of the cupboard.

A door leading out into the garage was off the same landing that led to the basement steps. Dee heard the 'whir' of the automatic garage door opener as they started down.

'Is that Dad?'

'Maybe. Oops. There they go,' said Dee, grabbing at Doug as the lights went out. This time, they didn't come on again. 'Come on, bud. We're going down. Give me the light.'

Reluctantly, Doug gave Dee the flashlight and dropped back. As she illuminated the stairs, he was right behind her, a death grip on her shirt. Assuming his imagination was working overtime fleshing out the details of Alice's wild tale, Dee tried to reassure him. 'Alice is a tease. You shouldn't let her get to you.'

'It could have been a dungeon,' he insisted. 'It was built a long, long time ago.'

'Dungeons belong to the dark ages, Doug. This house was built in the sixties during the Cold War,' Dee tried to reassure him.

'The what?'

'Cold War. When Russia and America had missiles pointing at one another.' Their footsteps rang in the quiet basement. Dee flicked the beam toward her father's workshop to the left of the stairs, then went on to repeat what her father'd told her about the storm shelter when she wasn't much bigger than Doug. Extending several feet from the basement wall, with the same dimensions of the port one storey up, the small narrow room was intended as a fall-out shelter in the event of a nuclear disaster. The thick walls and absence of windows made it the safest place to be in a storm. Though her aversion to the place was based mainly on the spider and centipede population, Dee wasn't without sympathy for Doug. She didn't lose patience, even though he balked in the open doorway of the shelter.

'Give me the light,' he said. 'I'm going to the spare bedroom instead. Or maybe I'll crawl under Dad's workbench.'

'This is better,' Dee said firmly. 'No windows to break.'

'How long do we have to stay?'

'Just until the wind quits blowing.' Dee brushed off a gallon paint can and sat down. 'I'll bet Great-great-great Gram Pru would've thought this was a pretty cushy place to sit out a storm.'

Doug shrank against her as volleys of thunder carried on like a shouting match.

Dee put an arm around him, adding, 'Pru tells about getting caught in a storm out on the open plains. They could see the storm coming. Guess the lightning forking down from those rolling black clouds was pretty scary. There wasn't any cover at all, nothing but grass for miles and miles.'

'Not even trees?'

'Nope. Besides, you aren't supposed to get under a tree in a storm. It might get hit by lightning,' Dee reminded. 'That's what scared Pru and her family so. They were sitting ducks. They just had to hunker down and take it. The hail beat the daylights out of the canvas covers and some of the animals were so scared, they broke free and ran off.'

'Did they get lost?'

'Some did. It took the men the better part of a day to round them up again.'

'Did they find them all?'

'Yes. Pru's family's cow was dead, though. Struck by lightning.'

'Really?'

Dee nodded. 'Pru was bummed over that. They depended on the cow for milk.'

'So they had to buy it at the store, huh?'

Dee smiled, but was spared an explanation by slow, uneven footsteps following light quick ones down the stairs. Realizing it was Mom and Alice, not Dad, who'd come home, she hurried to the foot of the stairs and shone her light up. Beside her, Doug blinked and covered his face as an answering beam shone right in his eyes. Red-faced and breathless from dragging her cast down the stairs, Mom panted, 'I tried to call. When no one answered, I thought we'd better come home and make sure you two were okay.'

'We went out with Georgia for Cokes,' Dee explained.

'All this for nothing. Look at us! We're drenched!' Alice squeezed rainwater from her hair.

'Did you walk home?' asked Doug.

'Don't be a doughface! The lights went out before the garage door was open far enough to get the car inside. I had to run inside and lift the door manually so Mom could get in without getting her cast wet.'

95

Dee's mother jumped at a loud crack of thunder. 'This storm isn't over yet. In the shelter. Hurry up, kids,' she urged.

'She's freaked. Aren't you, Mom?' Alice cheered up a bit.

'Who wouldn't be?' her mother snapped. 'The sky's green and the clouds are boiling. Half-way across the basement, she froze in her tracks. 'Listen!'

Dee's ears were already tuned to the agonizing, bone-crunch sound. A splintering crash followed. Over the howling wind was an aftermath of snapping and crackling. Dee was half-way up the stairs before she realized her mother was yelling at her to come back. Alice was right behind her, pushing.

'You two don't take another step! That was a tree! It may have brought power lines down with it and I don't like the sound of that wind!' Mom's voice pealed in a pitch to match the thunder.

Alice pushed at Dee's back. 'It couldn't have hit our house, it would have shaken the place to the foundations.'

'What about Michael?' cried Dee.

Mom hobbled to the basement window to check. Dee's pulses quickened at her stunned grasp. 'What is it, Mom?'

'The maple tree! It's. . .'

Dee whirled around, nearly dropping the flashlight as she bumped into Alice on her way back down. The window was high along the basement wall. She had to stand on tiptoe. The day was dark as dusk and rainwater was pouring into the window well, making the glass murky. But it looked like the roots of a tree sticking up, forming a barricade between their house and Michael's.

'I can't see!' Heart in her throat, Dee released the window latch. Unwittingly she pulled it open to a face full of muddy water. The wind was screaming, the rain lashing against the house, and the tree. . .the red maple. . .it'd smashed right into Michael's house!

'Call 9-1-1!'

Alice jumped to obey, but Mom, already on her way, called back, 'I'm going. You kids stay right here. Do you hear me! Right here!'

Dee grabbed a ladder from Dad's workshop to the left of the stairs. She dragged it to the window, climbed up, slid the window off the track and handed it down to Alice.

'Where're you going?' Alice cried.

Holding the flashlight, Doug pleaded, 'Dee, don't!'

Dee scarcely heard. The space where the window had been was tight, the window well beyond it further complicating her effort. Oblivious to bumps, scrapes, and concrete burns, she had nearly wriggled through when Alice grabbed her ankles and refused to let go.

'It's too dangerous, Dee.'

'Let go!' Dee tried to kick loose.

Alice clung all the tighter, yelling, 'Do you want

to get killed? Holler at him first, you idiot! See if he'll answer!'

Michael stared in numb disbelief at tree-tops gouging through the wall which'd separated Grandpa's room from the living-room. The leaves quaked and dripped and the floor beneath his feet groaned as the crash reverberated through the house in quivering aftershocks. The flimsier branches continued to twitch as the echoes faded and the dampness settled a thin mist of demolition dust. Michael drew a ragged breath. Only moments ago, he'd responded to an inner voice much stronger than intuition – a clear, two-worded message: *Get Grandpa!* The unspoken words were so compelling, he'd fled the window where he'd been watching the storm unleash its fury. He'd roused Grandpa from a nap and hustled him beneath the old upright piano, the heaviest piece of furniture in the house.

'What, what, what, what?' Grandpa babbled.

Michael was so dazed himself, it was hard to separate his trembling from Grandpa's. The whole house could come down around them yet. He waited a moment, then began inching from beneath the piano. 'Wait right there, Grandpa.'

'No, no, no, no, no!' Grandpa clutched at Michael, his eyes wide with terror.

'Easy. I'm not leaving you,' Michael turned back to soothe him. 'You're all right. I'm right here. I'll take care of you.'

The air coming in from outside was cold and damp. He grabbed an afghan off the nearby sofa, draped it around Grandpa's thin shoulders and urged him to stretch out facing the piano, his back to the destruction. Giving him a sofa pillow to clutch, he kept a reassuring hand on his back until he grew calmer, then eased slowly away, edging closer to the scene of devastation.

The wind shrilled through the gaping hole in the wall like deranged laughter. It tore a curtain loose and ripped a calender off the wall. Grandpa's bed was in fragments, the mattress and box springs flattened against the ruptured floor. Part of the roof had torn away. Beyond a jagged skylight of tattered plaster, splintered timber and shingle, lightning pierced angry banks of clouds.

An icy chill raced up his spine. No way could Grandpa have survived this! If not for those two unspoken words. Two words he might easily have ignored . . . 'Get Grandpa!' Michael's nerves jumped at the sound of his name echoing somewhere beyond the house.

'Michael? Michael! Can you hear me?'

Dee! He could hear her through the hole in the wall. But there was no way to reach the hole with the tree filling the room. He raced to his own bedroom. The damage, he noticed as he strode to the window, was relatively light. He took down the neon sign before opening the window. He lifted the screen, too. But it was dark as dusk and raining so hard, he couldn't see Dee.

'Dee? Where are you?' he yelled.

'Down here! The basement. Is anyone hurt?'

The trunk and the lower branches obscured Michael's view. Rain lashed his face as he leaned out the window, cupped his hand to his mouth and hollered back, 'No! We're okay.'

'Thank God! Mom's calling 9-1-1. I can come over if. . .'

'No, no! Stay put! Any damage over there?'

'We're fine so far. All but my ankles, anyway. Ouch! Alice, I'm not going anywhere. Would you quit gouging me!'

'Stop kicking!' Michael heard Alice retort. Those two, fighting in the midst of a tornado! Laughter bubbled, or was it hysteria? A black ooze from a dark, fearsome place? His teeth chattered. He was shaking so violently his spine hurt. He closed the window, dried his face on his shirt and hurried back to wait with Grandpa for the emergency crew to arrive.

Chapter 8

'Michael's house is a mess. Wiped out Mr Kolupa's room and part of the living room. Mr Kolupa was so upset, the emergency workers took him to the hospital just to be sure he didn't have a heart attack or something. Paula cried when she saw what the storm had done to her house. Michael looked like he could have cried, too, but he looked up the insurance adjuster's phone number for his mother instead. Once it quit raining, Dad started sawing up the tree. Michael and Doug and I helped while Mom went with Paula to the hospital to check on Mr Kolupa. Alice mobilized the neighborhood and before long, people were crowding all over the yard, wanting to help. You should have seen the look on that insurance man's face when he came and found that tree already cut into firewood, and Dad with a damage estimate prepared. He snapped his pictures and left while the neighbors helped Dad and Michael spread some tarps over the roof and that huge hole in the wall. It was getting dark by then and the power still wasn't on. Dad wouldn't let me open the refrigerator and with the stove being electric, the food options were pretty limited. I was riffling through the cupboards by flashlight, wondering how devilled ham on crackers with a dried apricot topping would be, when the doorbell rang. Alice'd ordered pizza. Sometimes she has a pretty cool head. She's also got a set of nails that could open cans. My ankles look like I got caught in a revolving door.

Anyway, some of the neighbors stayed and ate out on the deck. There's lines down everywhere. A guy across the street lost some shutters and shingles, another, a garden shed. But the major damage in our part of town was Michael's house.

Mom and Paula got home about the same time the power came on. Mr Kolupa was with them, but I think they gave him a sedative at the hospital, because he was pretty much zombified. Freaked Doug, having him under the same roof. Paula said they could go to a motel, but Mom wouldn't hear of it. She changed the sheets in Doug's room for Paula and freshened up the guest room in the basement for Mr Kolupa and Michael. Mr Kolupa climbed his apartment stairs for fifty years, so I guess stairs aren't a problem. Doug brought his sleeping bag in here with Alice and me. What with Mr Kolupa being down in the basement, he wouldn't let Alice turn the light off, which is why I'm still writing. He finally went to sleep. Alice has a pillow over her head, so I can't tell about her. She's quit clucking like a chicken anyway. Course there wouldn't be much point to it with Doug zonked out. I figure her

102

teasing is a cover for the fact she's pretty uncom-
fortable about Mr Kolupa being here, too.

Hearing Michael's truck start up out on the drive next door, Dee uncurled from the window-seat to douse the light. When she returned, all she could see was tail-lights disappearing down the street.

She tucked her journal away and slipped out of her room, fully dressed. Dad was snoring down the hall. But there was a light on in the kitchen. She found Mom and Paula at the table, teacups steaming between them. Paula's hair was still damp from the shower. It fell to her shoulders in loose ringlets, reminding Dee of Michael. His hair was short and light in color, but he had a similar fringe of curls at the back that spilled over his collar.

'The water's hot if you want some tea,' Dee's Mom offered.

'No, thanks. I heard Michael leave.' Dee swept her hair back and looked at Paula. 'How's he doing?'

'He's okay.' Paula overlapped her faded yellow robe across her ample bosom and added, 'And thanks, Dee, for asking. You've been a good friend.'

Paula was usually positive and self-sufficient. But tonight she looked pretty fragile. Afraid of saying the wrong thing, Dee angled her mother a glance for guidance. Mom nudged a chair with her foot.

'Sit down, Dee. You want some tea?'

Dee declined, but sliced two fresh peaches, drowned them in maple syrup and sprinkled some butter mints over the top. She set out dishes and spoons before joining the women at the table.

Paula curled one short, stout leg beneath her in the chair and helped herself to the peaches. She flashed Dee a faded smile. 'Interesting combination.'

'Dee comes up with some unique recipes.' Mom tried a second bite and added, 'I think you're on to something here, dear.'

Dee liked the combination, too. But her thoughts quickly tunneled back to her purpose in joining them. Adopting a casual tone, she asked, 'Did Michael go to Cheryl's house?'

Paula forked a peach slice and angled her a puzzled glance. 'You mean the redhead from Stevenson High? That was over weeks ago.'

'Oh. He's gone a lot in the evening and I just naturally thought. . .' Dee trailed off, chagrined at the relief she was feeling.

'He goes to Dad's tailor shop. Partly because of the flags. Partly because he needs some time to himself after spending his days with Dad.'

'Flags?' Dee echoed.

Paula nodded. 'Didn't he tell you? He's mending flags, just like Dad used to do.'

'Guess we haven't talked much lately,' Dee understated it.

'Michael's pretty tied down with Dad. It was his choice, being Dad's care-giver, I mean. But I'm wondering now if I shouldn't just put my foot down and insist it's too much.'

'What other options do you have, Paula?' Mom asked.

'Sheri and I talked about nursing home care weeks ago,' said Paula. 'But Michael was afraid Dad would be unhappy there. He wanted to bring him home with us. I've got to hand it to him, he's been very sweet with Dad. But I don't know how he's going to cope with the house in such a mess.'

'It won't take Bob long to get the house to the point where you can at least move back in,' Mom offered encouragement. 'You're welcome to stay here until then.'

'That's very sweet, but we can't impose on you like that. Particularly with Dad.' Paula sighed and added. 'There's nights when he hardly sleeps. I wouldn't want him disturbing you with his wandering.'

Dee asked, 'How come he doesn't sleep?'

'It's a common problem with Alzheimer's patients,' said Paula.

'Alzheimer's? Is that what's wrong with him?'

Paula nodded. She lifted her teabag out of her cup, caught it in the spoon and wrapped the string around it, squeezing out the excess liquid. 'I take it you've heard of it?'

'I've heard the name,' said Dee, though she knew too little about it even to ask questions.

'You saw how he was at graduation? How

childlike? That's a result of Alzheimer's. It kills brain cells.'

'Do they replenish?' asked Mom.

'No,' said Paula, eyes misting. 'It's a progressive thing, more and more cells dying, making the brain less and less able to do its job.'

'I'm so sorry,' said Mom.

Paula withdrew a tissue from the pocket of her robe. 'I didn't have any idea what we were in for when Dad was diagnosed as being in the middle stages. You know me! The problem-solver. I thought okay, so now we've got a name for it. Things seem less scary when they have names,' she added, drying her tears. 'Since then, I've read everything I could get my hands on. It isn't a rosy picture they paint. The disease is totally debilitating over the long term.'

'I had no idea, Paula,' murmured Mom. 'I've seen your Dad in the yard some, and visited with him a little. I figured he was getting forgetful, that's all.'

'You aren't too surprised by absentmindedness, I guess, as people get older. That's partly why Sheri and I were so slow to pick up on Dad's problem.' Paula's hands curled around the teacup. She sipped sparingly, then settled the cup in the saucer again. 'Recently, I've joined a support group for families of Alzheimer's patients. I've tried to get Michael to go, too. But he refuses. You know how stubborn he can be.'

'Why doesn't he want to go?' asked Dee.

'He can't see what good it would do to talk Dad's illness over with a bunch of people he doesn't know.'

'But if they're going through the same thing. . .' began Mom.

Paula lifted her shoulders, then let them fall in a gesture of defeat. 'I've tried to tell him it's not altogether the downer he thinks. The people are very kind. They have some good ideas, you know, just about coping day to day. Practical insights, that sort of thing.'

Dee averted her gaze, thinking of Michael. *He probably felt it would be a breach of loyalty to parade his grandfather's odd behavior before strangers. Not to mention embarrassing. That's how she'd feel, anyway.* Hesitantly, she asked, 'Can't the doctors do something?'

'No, Dee. There's no known cure.'

'What a shame,' said Mom. 'Your father's worked hard all his life. And he's such a gentle, sweet man. It must be very difficult.'

Paula's eyes filled again. 'As hard as it is for Sheri and me, I think it's even worse for Michael. Over the years, he's depended on Dad to be there when I couldn't. It's hitting him pretty hard.'

Mom reached over and patted Paula's hand, murmuring gentle words. Looking on, Dee asked, 'Is there something I can do?'

'It might help him to talk about it.' Paula's attempt at a smile wobbled. 'He trusts you, Dee. Just be there for him.'

Dee nodded, fresh understanding easing her hurt and confusion over graduation night, the key-chain fiasco and the distance Michael'd been keeping.

Concerned her father would be frightened should he awaken to find himself in a strange place, Paula went to the basement to wait for Michael's return. She took the battery-charged phone with her so she could call her sister.

Dee's mother went to bed. But Dee had too much to think about. While she understood Michael's reasons for wanting to keep his grandpa's disease private, she wondered if it was good for Mr Kolupa to be so isolated. Yet when he went out, embarrassing things happened. Like graduation. It was a tough call, for sure. Poor Michael. She really would like to help.

Just be there for him. Paula's words echoed.

But he'd not confided his trouble, nor indicated in any way that he wanted her help. Then again, if it were Sally or Georgia, she wouldn't wait to be asked, because sometimes, the asking was hardest when needed the most. Though, other times, friends plain didn't want you butting in, in which case you risked getting your feelings hurt. But, what were feelings measured against the pain of losing by degrees someone you loved?

Just be there for him.

Enough vacillating! Dee padded bare-footed to the landing and opened the door to the basement, thinking Paula would probably like to go to bed.

She could go down and sit with Mr Kolupa until Michael came home. Then they could talk.

But mid-way down, Dee's courage started to fade. *What if Mr Kolupa woke up and didn't recognize her? Would he be frightened? What was she supposed to do if he tried to wander away? What if Michael didn't want to talk?* Filled with misgivings, Dee retreated back up the stairs and was trying to find room in the refrigerator for the syrup when she heard the front door open, then quietly close again. The carpet absorbed the sound of Michael's footsteps, but the glass globe in the lamp by Dad's chair rattled as he passed.

'You the only one still up?' he asked from the doorway.

'Your Mom hasn't turned in yet.' Dee met his sleepy-eyed gaze. 'She's downstairs with your grandpa.'

He nodded as if to say he'd assumed as much. Elbows bent, fingertips reaching into his pockets, he looked past her to the yawning refrigerator door. 'Is it snack time?'

'Slim pickings, but I'll see what I can do,' Dee gathered some celery, a cucumber, olives, a package of dried beef and some low-fat cream cheese. Nudging the refrigerator door closed, she motioned toward the dishwasher. 'Grab a couple of plates out of there, would you?'

Michael lifted an eyebrow, suspicious of the armload she dumped on the table. 'You aren't going to use me for a guinea-pig, are you?'

'No, no. These are tried and true. Cukes, Canoes, and Beef Roll-ups. Doug calls them "Throw-ups". As he gobbles them down faster than I can roll them up.' She noticed a thin line on his cheek where a branch had snapped while they were cutting up the tree. It curved upward as he crossed to the sink to wash his hands. Definitely the makings of a smile.

Encouraged, Dee said, 'Green or black olives for your Canoes?'

'Surprise me.' He opened the dishwasher, slid the plates on to the table and sat down.

Over the years, dozens of times, Michael'd watched from their kitchen table while she raided the icebox and rummaged through the cupboards, throwing something together. But always before, they'd been at ease, talking, joking, even bickering. This time was different. He'd brought the night air on his skin and his fingers, as he turned the plate, were long and strong and capable-looking. She was aware of a pulse beat in her throat and the nerve-endings in her hands. They prickled like needles as she filled celery stalks with cream cheese and capped them with a mixture of green and black olives. Though she'd not spoken of it, not even in her diary, the tree that'd hit Michael's house had in a symbolic way hit her too. She'd been as scared as she'd ever been in her life. It was a revealing kind of fear, and when Michael's voice had finally come ringing back to her, she'd acknowledged with weak-kneed relief that a lot of the uneasiness and hurt and confusion she'd felt lately wasn't so much because she feared losing Michael's friendship. Rather, a defense mechanism. She was seeing him in a new way. A new person. With secrets and surprises and facets to his personality that intrigued. She wanted to know him more and that wanting made her vulnerable.

'They do look like canoes,' Michael broke the small silence. Rocking the celery strip between his fingers, he mused, 'And these little guys in red caps are doing the rowing.'

She answered his grin, singing, 'Michael rowed his boat ashore.'

He bit into the celery, taking down two rowers at once. 'Mmm. Not bad.'

'Told you so.' Dee rinsed her hands and brushed them across her jeans before spreading cream cheese on the dried beef. 'So how's the flag business?'

His blue gaze sharpened. 'Who told you about that?'

'I have my sources.'

'Mom, right?' He sounded pained. 'What else did she tell you?'

'Just that your attitude needs adjusting on account you weren't corrected enough as a child.' She arranged the beef bits on cucumber slices and slid some on to his plate.

'Quit being so smart and float me another Canoe.'

'Say please.'

His blue gaze caught hers and held. The ingredients came together just right and he smiled the nicest smile she'd seen from him in weeks. 'Please.'

There was a feather-duster cartwheeling down in her rib-cage. Trying not to give herself away, Dee passed him the plate and sat down across from him. Steering well away from any subject that might overload the mood, she nibbled celery and carried the conversation from Georgia leaving for camp in the morning, to Sally's tips, to Tulip getting the job *she'd* wanted.

Michael forced a Roll-up into a Canoe, a combination she hadn't considered. 'I could use an assistant, if you're looking for something besides babysitting.'

'Assistant?' Dee thought instantly of Mr Kolupa. Guardedly, she said, 'To help with your grandfather?'

'No, with the flags.' He bit into the double-decker canapé.

Dee brightened. 'Oh! The flags. Tell me about that.'

'Pretty simple, actually. There's a lot of flags flying in town. But the wind can whip them to ribbons if you don't catch them when they first start to fray. I got to thinking it'd be a good way to gather some cash for my neon shop. So I called all the flag-flying businesses and government offices. Offered a pick-up, repair, and return service.' He scraped the last of the cream cheese from his plate with a fork and licked it clean. 'Negative aspects aside –

such as trees on houses – storms can be your friend if you're in the flag-repair business.'

'I think you're on to something.'

Michael framed a lopsided grin. 'So, are you interested?'

'Sure!' said Dee, delighted. 'I should warn you, though. I'm not much of a seamstress.'

'Nothing to it but a straight cut and a hem-stitch. A trained monkey could do it.'

'Thank you, Michael. I'll try to live up to my predecessor.'

Grinning, he picked up an olive and drew back his hand as if he intended to launch it at her. They were both laughing when Paula came up the stairs.

Eyes red-rimmed and heavy-lidded, she squinted in the bright light. 'I thought I heard voices.' She touched Michael's arm. 'Guess the sedative worked. Dad's sleeping soundly.'

'He's had a rough day.'

'We all have.' Paula closed the gap in her robe with one hand and shrugged the kinks from her shoulders. 'I'm going to get some sleep. We've got decisions to make tomorrow.'

'Decisions?' echoed Michael. His face tensed. 'About the house, you mean?'

'I was thinking about Dad, but yes, the house, too.'

'You don't have to worry about Grandpa. I'm going to take a few things over to the apartment in the morning. We can stay there until the house is finished.' He came out of his chair as if he were eager to settle all questions right now.

But his mother turned away, insisting, 'We'll talk about it tomorrow.'

Silence settled between them once Paula had gone. Dee felt the ground she'd covered by Canoe and Cuke and Roll-up, slipping away as Michael drew back into his shell. She could see that Paula was right, he *did* need to open up and talk about the tough time he'd been having accepting Mr Kolupa's illness. Uncertain how to go about drawing him out, Dee put the lid on the olives. 'Michael? Could I ask you about your grandpa?' she ventured.

'What about him?'

Dee kept her voice low and her eyes down. 'Just. . .about him.'

It grew so quiet she could hear her heart beat, the clock tick and the water heater kick on in the utility closet. Michael crossed to the sink and turned on the tap. Just when she thought he wouldn't answer at all, he asked, 'Do you remember your first day at school?'

'Just that I was scared,' she said, thinking back. 'Mom couldn't stay and I didn't know anyone.'

'Strangers in a strange building where you don't know your way around.' He returned to the table with a glass of water, and stood there with his hand around it. 'Lots of choices, like which door and which coat hook and which desk and which book and where is the bathroom? And you're afraid to ask questions, because maybe you've already been

114

told, and if you ask, someone might get after you? Right?'

'Something like that,' she said, though it would seem his recall was much better than hers.

Michael drained the glass in six swallows and set it down again. 'Every day is like that for Grandpa. Any more questions?'

Though he hadn't raised his voice, it had an edge that stung like flying glass. Dee flushed at having overstepped a forbidden boundary. She wagged her head no.

'I think I'll turn in, then.'

Dee blinked a couple of times and didn't catch another breath until she heard him start down the stairs. She wanted to help. She really did. But he didn't want to talk, and she didn't know how to make him. Besides, he had Paula and her sister Sheri and her husband. Plus, he had a spiritual thing going for him. He wasn't outspoken about it, but he drew strength from it, she could tell. So maybe Paula was wrong. Maybe he didn't need so much to open up, as time to work things through.

Until then, she had a feeling a lot of things were on hold. Herself, included. It made for insecure feelings. Big-time vulnerability. Remembering a particular entry in Pru's journal, Dee found the worn leather-bound book in her dark room. She curled up in her favorite chair to read again words that aroused a sympathetic kinship.

We reached Ft Kearney along the Platte River this morning. Father restocked supplies while

Mother, who has been ill, spent the day resting. Tonight after supper, everyone in the train gathered around a common campfire. There was a lot of talking, some fiddle playing and some dancing. I sneaked a glance at Seth Hickman. He winked, just as bold as you please. But he didn't ask me to dance. Just as well. My feet were too battered from walking to be trampled on by the likes of him.'

As if she didn't care, when clearly she did. When had the pretending turned to admission for Pru? Obviously it had, or she never would have become Pru Morris Hickman. Dee itched to thumb ahead in search of romantic interludes, but resisted the temptation, resolving instead to worry about her own love life. For the pretending was over where she was concerned. There was relief in simply admitting how much she cared for Michael, even if it did make her vulnerable.

Chapter 9

'I didn't tell Mom what a close call it was with Grandpa today. But you know and I know that it was You who saved his life. I can't quite figure out why, because it seems like the tree would have been quicker and kinder than this downhill slide. For Grandpa, anyway. But you said 'Get Grandpa' and I got him and I'm glad I did. Coming that close to losing him made me realize that I'm not near ready to let him go. So thank You for sparing him.'

Michael couldn't type the words into his computer tonight. He thought them instead as he stretched out on the cot Dee's mom had put up for him in the basement bedroom. He could hear Grandpa in the bed a few feet away, thumping his foot in his sleep. He'd done that for years, even when he napped on the sofa. 'He thinks he's Peter Cotton Tail,' Gram used to say when he was small and Grandpa would thump his foot like that. Her eyes would twinkle, and she'd put a finger to her lip warning him not to giggle too loudly.

Michael's mouth curved in the darkness as those good times embraced him. Gram and Dad still with them, and Grandpa healthy and strong. Special times a long time ago. Made safe by his ignorance that death could hit like a lightning bolt. In looking back, it seemed as if those days had flowed together into a golden seamless 'before'. Then Gram and Dad had died within months of one another, and even though he accepted Grandpa's explanation that they were in a place called heaven and that they could be reunited some day, it didn't change the void in his life or the anguish of missing them. Their deaths blurred into one dark sad lonely winter. But grief eased like a broken bone or a wound slowly healing until thoughts of them brought comfort, even laughter in place of the pain. If it helped him to remember those good times – and it did – then maybe the past being more real than the present was, to Grandpa, a kindness heaven-sent. He would remind himself of that when Grandpa mistook him for Richard, when Richard was young and exasperating. Or when he mistook Mom for Gram.

Too tired to think ahead to tomorrow and the challenges presented by the storm damage, Michael rolled off the cot and pushed it against the door so the only way out was over him. He didn't want Grandpa wandering in the night, disrupting Dee's family.

He curved an arm under his pillow, and let his mind wander to Dee. He'd enjoyed sitting at the table as she pottered around the kitchen. You couldn't call it cooking, exactly, not when it started

118

with ready-made stuff. Even when they were small, and in the Kool-Aid stand business, Dee insisted on decorating the glasses with orange or lemon slices. She'd experimented on them too, trying to improve upon what needed no improvement, an opinion he'd voiced as he sampled cookies dripping with honey and jam. 'Quit eating them if you don't like my recipe!' she'd ordered with a sniff. He closed heavy lids and sighed. These days, plain old saltines and water would be good with those dusky gray eyes and that tempting mouth smiling at him across the table. He wished she hadn't asked about Grandpa, though. He was afraid he'd been abrupt with her. Not that he'd intended it that way – his emotions were close to the surface these days. Bearing down, trying to keep them from blowing, he wasn't as careful choosing words as he might be.

Mom's quiet knocking awakened Michael the next morning. He lifted his head off the pillows to see Grandpa snapping his suspenders on over his yesterday's undershirt. The pants were yesterday's too, as were the socks. Stiff from a night on the narrow cot, Michael pulled on his jeans, jerked the cot out of the way, and opened the door for his mother.

She'd been over to the house and had brought back clean clothes for both of them. Her face fell when she saw Grandpa. Once he was dressed, it was difficult to convince him he needed to shower and change into clean clothes. She eased into it, saying, 'I brought you some clothes, Dad. See? Your blue shirt. It goes very well with these trousers. But you'll have to shower first.'

'I did,' he said.

'You just got up. You haven't had time to shower,' Mom reasoned.

Michael took the armload of clothes and set them on the bed. 'Let it go, Mom, I'll help him. You're going to be late for work.'

'I called them and told them I wouldn't be in today. I'm taking Dad visiting.'

'Visiting?' Michael paused in folding the cot. 'Visiting *who*?'

'Rosewood Health Care.'

The nursing home thing again! 'Mom,' he began, but she cut him short with a wave of her hand.

'I called Sheri last night. We had a long talk about Rosewood's special unit for. . .' She stepped aside, letting Grandpa out of the room, then turned so she could keep her eye on him as he began a slow inspection of the cinder-block wall. Quietly, she finished, '. . .Alzheimer's patients.'

'What is this. . .this. . .?' asked Grandpa, turning back.

'We're in the Findleys' basement, Dad,' said Mom.

He scratched his bald head, a fretful frown forming. 'Is it gaol?'

'Dad, it's a basement.'

'Where's the. . .the things. . .the door things? Get the key, Stella.'

'There was a storm yesterday, remember? A tree hit the house. We're staying with neighbors,' Mom reminded him.

Michael could tell by Grandpa's befuddled expression he didn't remember the storm or the tree or why they were here. Maybe it was better that way.

'Get the. . .thing. The. . .thing. The door lock, the door key.'

'In your pocket, Grandpa,' said Michael. 'Put your hand in your pocket. The other pocket.'

Grandpa found the right pocket and pulled out the old set of keys Doug had reluctantly relinquished. He continued along the wall, tracing a mortar line between blocks with one of the keys.

Watching him, Mom said in a low voice, 'He didn't get up in the night, did he?'

Michael wagged his head. 'Whatever they gave him at the hospital knocked him out pretty good.' He paused, searching for words to make her understand about Grandpa and nursing homes. 'He's got a thing about gaol. That's where he'll think he is if you put him in one of those places.'

'I don't like it any better than you do, but we're short on options.' She kept her voice low.

'I said I'd keep him for the summer and that's what I'm going to do.'

'That was before the storm, Michael. We have no power next door and no hot water. We can't bathe, we can't cook, and there's a hole in the wall large enough to drive a truck through.' Mom stood her guard. 'Not to mention the commotion of hammers and saws buzzing all over the place. Dad couldn't stand that. Sheri doesn't have room, and we can't impose further on the Findleys.'

Even if they could impose, Michael was concerned that the stress of unfamiliar surroundings would cause Grandpa to act out in strange ways. 'What about Grandpa's apartment? Like I said last night, we can stay there until the house is fixed.'

'It's a good temporary solution for the two of us,' agreed Mom. 'But if we move Dad in, we'll have to go through the whole ordeal of moving him out again when the repair work is done. You know how devastating that move was to him the first time. He hasn't recovered yet.'

That hard-worn peace that'd filled Michael so briefly last night was burning off fast. He felt the tension of past weeks gather in his shoulders. 'Sounds to me like you've already made up your mind.'

'I guess I have,' she admitted. 'Rosewood is the most practical solution for the time being.'

Michael jutted out his chin. 'Just because it's practical doesn't mean it's what's best.'

'This is agonizing for me, too,' Mom said quietly. 'But I've been on the phone with the administrator, explaining the situation. She was very reassuring. They have a room available. We have a ten o'clock appointment. I'd like you to come too.'

'What's the point?' he asked, frustration rising.

'I want you to see the place and be assured he'll be okay.'

Michael crammed his bare feet into his high tops, jerked a clean shirt over his head, and started up the steps without answering.

'Michael, wait a minute. I wasn't finished,' Mom called after him.

'They're warehouses, Mom. For worn-out, used-up people,' he spat, the bitter words burning his throat, his gut, behind his eyes.

'Michael. . .'

'Forget it! I'm not going. Not today, not tomorrow, not ever!'

He pushed the screen open at the top of the stairs and tore out through the Findleys' garage. He wouldn't, either. He couldn't bear to see them shuffle Grandpa around like a stick of furniture. Strangers who wouldn't care he'd once been the best tailor downstate. Or that he liked mayonnaise on his eggs. Or that 'Till I Waltz Again with You' made him cry. How could Mom do it? How could she?

Daylight was flooding through the curtains when Dee awoke. She raised up on her elbow to see Doug holding himself and dancing from foot to foot. 'What's the matter?'

'I've got to go.'

By the look of his pajama fronts, he'd wet in the night. 'Is Alice camped in the bathroom again?'

He shook his head.

'Then what're you waiting for?'

'Come with me, okay?' he asked.

Remembering Mr Kolupa, Dee saved her breath and swung her legs out of bed. Padding barefoot to the threshold, she waved him on. The flannel lining in his sleeping bag had done a job on his hair. It looked like whipped foam on a rootbeer float.

He stopped and looked back. 'Aren't you coming?'

'Go on. I'll stand right here in the door,' she promised. 'Brush your hair while you're in there.'

He raced down the hall, did his bathroom business, and came out making faces as he dragged a brush through his tangles. On the way to his bedroom, he looked back over his shoulder to make sure she was still watching.

'Knock first, just in case Paula's still sleeping,' warned Dee.

He peeked instead, then threw the door open wide. Dee could see the neatly made bed. Doug turned back and entreated, 'Wait, okay?'

'I'm right here, Doug.' It was going to be a long day if Doug refused to let her out of his sight for fear of Mr Kolupa. But she waited, and when he came back he was fully dressed. He wadded the rubber sheet that'd been under his sleeping bag into the bag and stuffed the whole works into the corner.

He'd worked hard to overcome his bed-wetting. The accident was his first setback in a couple of weeks. 'You should have called me, Doug. I'd have gone with you.'

He kept his head down. 'I tried to wake up. I thought I walked into the bathroom and lifted the lid. It seemed so real. But I guess I dreamed it.'

'No big deal. I'm going to get dressed and fix us some breakfast, then I'll wash everything up. Looks like the alarm clock has stopped. Feels late, though.'

Doug pulled out the old pocket watch, looked at it closely and said in a serious voice, 'Six o'clock.'

Dee knew better. The watch was just as broken as the day Paula had given it to him and Alice's bed was empty. She and Mom must all be at work by now. She grabbed cut-off shorts and her Hard Rock Café T-shirt and dashed for the bathroom, leaving Doug in her room, peering into the rose bowl. The water was black now, and there was very little left of the petals. But so far, she couldn't be persuaded to throw it away.

Dee showered and dressed quickly. Doug was camped right outside the bathroom door. She nearly tripped over him on her way out. Annoyed, she pointed out, 'You could be worrying for nothing, Doug. The house is awfully quiet. I'm not even sure Mr Kolupa's here.'

'Really?' A tooth was starting to show where a week ago there'd been only a space. He explored its edge with the tip of his tongue. 'You could go see.'

'I'm fixing breakfast,' Dee said firmly.

Doug trailed her to the kitchen. 'Will you have to feed him if he's here?'

'I don't *have* to, but I will because I want to.'

'If he's here, I'll have my cereal in my room.'

Dee sighed and caved in. 'All right, all right, I'll go see.' She returned to her bedroom for the sleeping bag, first. That way, if she bumped into Michael, she'd have a reason, beyond Mr-Kolupa-scouting, for being down there.

The laundry room was down the stairs to the right, the bathroom right next door. She could hear the shower running as she stuffed the sleeping bag into the washing-machine. Uncertain whether it was Mr Kolupa or Michael showering, Dee set the machine. She was on her way back to the stairs when Paula's voice drifted to her from the bedroom.

Reasoning she must have taken the day off, Dee approached the open door. Paula was alone, her back to the door. 'No, Sheri. I haven't changed my mind. It's just that Michael was awfully upset. He won't even go with me to check the place out.'

Hearing her voice break, Dee backed away, moving soundlessly toward the stairs. 'I don't want to take Dad alone,' she heard Paula say. 'Can't you get a sitter?'

Where was Michael? Why was he upset? And where was Paula taking her dad? Anxious not to get caught in the middle of a family thing, Dee retreated up the stairs. Doug wanted a 'toad-in-the-hole' for breakfast. She'd heated the skillet, cut the center out of a piece of bread and was breaking the egg into the hole when Paula came up the stairs.

126

She greeted them both, but turned down Dee's breakfast offer, saying she and her father had an appointment and that they would stop for breakfast on the way. Her eyes were a little red, but she seemed fine otherwise.

'I've got to run home for Dad's medical records,' said Paula, turning back at the door. 'Dad's downstairs getting dressed. I don't think he'll come up, but if he does, will you make sure he doesn't get out of the house, Dee?'

Dee nodded agreement and didn't ask how she was supposed to stop him if he tried. Fortunately, Paula was back right away, this time with the car. She went back downstairs, and when she came up, Mr Kolupa came with her. Clean-shaven and neat in dark trousers, a pale blue dress shirt and his felt hat, he broke into a smile at the sight of Doug.

'Michael!' he said with gentle pleasure.

Doug's jaw dropped. He froze, fork half-way to his mouth.

'No, Dad,' Paula said quickly. 'It's Doug. Doug Findley.'

Mr Kolupa paid her no heed. He circled the table and patted Doug's arm. 'See how you've grown! He's a fine boy, Stella. A fine boy.'

He kept patting and praising, praising and patting, while Doug sank lower and lower in his chair until his chin slipped beneath the table top.

Seeing Doug's distress, Paula offered Mr Kolupa her arm and distracted him, saying, 'Tell him good-bye. Dad. We have visiting to do.'

Mr Kolupa gave Doug one last pat, then took Paula's arm. 'We're going. . .you know. . .' he moved his feet.

'Dancing?' guessed Dee, and he beamed as he turned away.

Doug's gaze followed the old man to the door. He straightened cautiously, like a snail with its feelers out. At length, he let out a long breath and whispered, 'Who is 'Stella'?'

'That was Michael's grandmother. Mr Kolupa's wife. She died a long time ago.' Dee poured herself a glass of juice.

'He called me Michael.'

'I heard.' Dee sipped her juice.

'Why'd he call me that?'

'He remembers Michael being small, and you fill the bill.'

Doug studied her response a moment, then ventured, 'Do I look like Michael?'

'No. But I guess that doesn't matter. He's confused, Doug. What's in his head is what's real to him.'

Doug twisted his mouth to one side. 'How can that be?'

Dee thought it over a moment. 'Remember last night when you tried to wake up, and you were trying so hard, you dreamed you were awake and in the bathroom?'

'And I wet?'

'Right. Did it seem real to you at the time?'

He nodded.

'That's the way it is with Mr Kolupa.'

'But when I woke up, I knew it was a dream.'

'That's the difference right there,' said Dee.

Doug picked up the little round hole of toast she'd fried separately and nibbled mouse-sized bites until it was gone. 'What can we do?' he asked at length.

'I don't think there's anything that'll help, Doug. Sometimes people get sick and it just isn't fixable.'

'So they die?' At her nod, he asked, 'Is Mr Kolupa going to die?'

'No, no. I don't think so. Not for a long time, anyway,' she said quickly, though she had no basis for such a diagnosis.

Doug picked the watch out of his pocket and laid it on the table next to his plate. He finished his breakfast in silence. Dee's thoughts drifted to Michael. Could he have gone to his grandfather's shop? No harm in checking.

Doug jumped at the chance to take the city bus downtown. They got off at the stop nearest Mom's antique shop. Mom was surprised to see them. But she seemed to sense it was more than boredom that'd brought Dee downtown. She found something simple for Doug to 'fix'. Leaving him in the back shop, she led the way out front, asking quietly, 'Is something wrong?'

Dee repeated what she'd overheard in the basement and asked if she knew what Paula had in mind for Mr Kolupa. Her mother told her about the nursing home with a special Alzheimer's wing.

Understanding now why Michael was upset, Dee left Doug with her mother and set off for Mr Kolupa's tailor shop just a couple of blocks away.

The front door was locked. Dee slipped down the alley and tried the side door. The knob turned beneath her hand. The blended odor of machine oil, sweeping compound, dust and old bricks washed over her as she let herself in. The lights were out in the back room. What little sunshine filtered through the high, dingy alley windows was pale and thin. Hesitating just inside the door, Dee called Michael's name.

She heard chair legs scrape the wooden floor and spotted him slumped in front of a machine, his back to her. There was a flag draped through the machine and over his lap, but he wasn't sewing. Nor did he turn to face her. *Had he come here to cry?* Heat swept up her neck, uncertainty gnawed at her stomach. What could she say to make him feel better? There were no such words. As the silence stretched out, Dee crossed the room on soundless steps. Feeling gauche, bumbling, inadequate, she started to lay a hand on his shoulder. But just short of touching, she remembered graduation night, and how uncomfortable things had gotten when she'd tried to comfort him. Wishing their relationship hadn't become so delicate, she murmured his name.

Voice thick and low, he asked, 'Did Mom take him?'

'Yes.' Dee swallowed hard as he sat motionless,

his shoulders bunched. 'I'd help if I could.'

'Nothing to do, once she pulls rank,' he said in the same dull tone.

It was defeat to him. Bitter defeat. Dee'd never felt so helpless. Palms perspiring, pulse pounding at her temples, she retreated a step. 'Listen, I didn't mean to intrude. I'll head back down the street. If you need anything, I'll be at Granny's Attic.'

Mutely, he nodded.

Dee made for the door and was letting herself out when the chair scraped again.

'Dee?'

She paused and turned back to see Michael standing by the machine. The light was dim, his features dark planes and shadows. Throat aching, she waited as he dragged the flag off the machine and held it loosely.

'I've got some stuff to do,' he said finally. 'But drop back by after a while if you want to.'

It wouldn't qualify as opening up by a long shot. But at least it wasn't rejection. Lifting her hand, Dee called, 'Later, then,' and slipped out the door.

Chapter 10

'Dear Georgia,

I remember from last year that at mail call they make you sing a song for every letter you get. Knowing how shy you are (yuk, yuk) I'll try to make it worth your suffering the torments of stage fright. The storm yesterday dropped a tree on Michael's house. It knocked a hole in the roof and the wall and pretty well demolished Mr Kolupa's bedroom. They spent the night at our house, but this morning, Paula took Mr Kolupa to Rosewood. I don't know if he's staying indefinitely, or if he's coming back as soon as the house is repaired. Dad's going to do the repairs.

Guess what? Michael's started a flag repair business and he's asked me to help. Yes, all-thumbs-with-a-needle me. The coolest thing about it is gives me time with Michael. Feel free to read between the lines. Or, better yet, I'll just come out and say it – I've got a thing for him. I haven't told Sally – she's the first to admit she's lousy at keeping secrets, and this is definitely a secret. At least until I find out if it's going anywhere.

I hope you're having fun and meeting lots of cute guys. Stay out of the poison ivy and don't let the bears nibble your toes. Can't wait to hear from you.'

Dee signed the letter and found an envelope in her mother's desk. She marked through 'Granny's Attic' and wrote her own return address. Glancing at her watch, she figured she'd have to kill another half an hour before she could return to Mr Kolupa's shop. Better make it an hour – give Michael plenty of time to get himself together. Poor guy, he'd tried so hard to take care of his grandfather. Too bad the tree messed things up for him. Though the real shame, of course, was his grandfather sickness. *Alzheimer's.* Even the name sounded formidable.

Michael sat in the darkness, elbows on his knees, head in his hand, bemoaning his luck. *Find a dark hole and let loose, and who comes along but Dee? Can't buy a break these days! What's the verse Grandpa says over and over – Oh wretched man that I am, who will release me from this body of death. . .' That's what I need, some release. It is death, this whole life. Not just people breathing a last breath, but Grandpa walking around with his brain dying bit by bit. Mom at me, and me at Mom. And Aunt Sheri so wrapped up, Dr Death could be on the staff at Rosewood, and she wouldn't squawk, just so long as it didn't inconvenience her. On and on, with no let up in sight. I wish I could get in my truck and take off. Just drive away and leave it all behind.*

He wrestled raw feelings without resolving much of anything. But there remained that seed of faith planted in childhood by a man he trusted. What was there to do but plod on? He went upstairs to splash water on his hot face and air out the apartment. He was sweeping the cobwebs out of the black iron grate in the floor when Dee's voice wafted up from downstairs.

'Michael? Are you busy?'

'Upstairs, Dee.'

Following the sound of his voice, she paused beneath the grate one storey below and listed her face.

'Look out for the dust.'

She backed away, brushing slim arms. 'What're you doing up there?'

'Sweeping.'

'You must be related to Alice. She's never heard of a dustpan, either.'

He sneezed his lungs free of dusty air and invited, 'Come on up.'

Dee was still raking her fingers through her hair as she came in through the dingy kitchen. 'Anything crawling on me?'

'Not that I can see.'

'That's because you're not looking,' she accused.

He was too looking – just not for spiders. Clad in cut-off shorts and a T-shirt with a scarf in her hair, she was by her presence ushering rays of light through the dark haze of his thoughts. Afraid he was going to make a fool of himself if he didn't *stop* looking, he pushed the broom into her hands. 'Here, since you're the expert.'

'We aren't working on flags?'

'Later, maybe. I've got some moving to do first. Mom and I are going to stay here until the house is done,' he answered her puzzled expression.

'Oh. I didn't realize.'

'You don't have to help if you don't want to,' he added.

'I don't mind. I've got to go back to the shop and get Doug pretty soon, though.'

'That's okay. We'll put him to work, too.'

Dee followed him deeper into the apartment. 'I haven't been up here in years. It seemed so huge when we were kids.'

The kitchen and bathroom were closed in, but the rest was open space. Wood-framed partitions on wheels divided two bedrooms from the living area. The privacy was limited, as the partitions lacked several feet of reaching the ceiling. Years ago, Michael's mother had replaced the wallpaper on the partitions. But with only the most basics in furnishing left, the place was pretty bare and shabby-looking.

Neat as she was, Dee had noticed. But she was polite enough not to comment. Her footsteps scraped across the grate in the floor. She tapped him with the broom. 'Remember that old woman, shaking her umbrella at us when we spied from here on your grandpa's prayer meeting?'

'I'd forgotten,' said Michael, though it came

back at her prompting.

Her dimples flashed. 'I think about it every time I see your grandpa rearranging chairs out on the deck.'

Heat swept up Michael's neck. He'd wondered and wondered at Grandpa's strange linking of Scripture and chairs, and here Dee had hit on the explanation without conscious effort. All those years of meetings. *Would there be chairs for him at Rosewood?* He set his chin. It was up to Mom to tell him. He wasn't going to give her any more grief over her decision. But he wasn't going to support it either. Nor was he setting foot in Rosewood.

Dee's face turned hot the minute the mention of Mr Kolupa's thing with chairs flew out of her mouth. Michael didn't break down or get defensive, but still, it was awkward. She was glad when they locked the place up and drove to his house. They salvaged what they could from the refrigerator on the first trip, then stopped for Doug on their second pass.

Alice was climbing the corporate ladder at Granny's Attic waiting on customers while Mom dusted. Give her her dues, she had the finesse of a natural-born sales person. 'Oh, yes! That'll be just purrrfect for your little granddaughter,' she gushed to the white-haired customer considering a Shirley Temple doll.

Dee collected Doug from the back room and filled Mom in on their plans.

'Say, if there's room in Michael's truck, how

about bringing the mirror from your bedroom? I've got space for it now,' said Mom.

Dee had grown attached to the mirror and hated to give it up. 'I use it every day, Mom. It's such a neat old piece. Can't I keep it?'

'I like most of the things that come through this shop. But we're in the business of selling. It's no good getting attached to the merchandise.' Mom held a firm line.

'I know, I know.' Dee had heard it all before.

Dee and Doug trekked out to the curb where Michael was waiting. Doug tumbled into the truck, taking the middle seat. Dee climbed in after him.

'It's funny Alice can talk her way from dusting to sales clerk, and I can't even talk Mom out of a mirror,' she grumbled.

'It was on loan,' chirped Doug.

'So are we. We better watch it, hanging around that shop,' warned Dee.

Doug giggled, knowing it was a joke. But Michael said morosely, 'We're all on loan.'

She rolled her eyes. 'Thanks for shedding that cheery light.'

'Watch out for the girl!' warned Doug.

Dee braced her right hand against the dash and flung a protective left arm across Doug as Michael hit the brakes and screeched to a halt two feet from the broad palm of Tulip Johnson's uplifted hand. She was wearing bright green leggings and an orange top too long for a shirt, too short for a dress. Her feet were firmly planted in the middle of their lane of traffic, her filmy orange garb billowing in the breeze like petals. Perspiration glistened on her freckle-burnished countenance as she gave them a cheerful wave.

'Thanks, Mikey. Mr Oppenheimer left his wallet over there and we're over here, worried the hooligans will find it first.'

With that she turned and beckoned to a shrunken little man waiting on the curb. He came on a shuffling gait and linked his frail arm with her sturdy one.

'Hooligans?' Doug followed the odd couple's ponderous parade across the street, beneath the shade of a striped awning and into Livingston's Variety Store. 'What's a holigan?'

'That's just Tulip being weird,' said Dee.

Michael shifted and let out the clutch. 'She's colorful, for sure.'

'I know what color, too. Orange!' said Doug.

Dee laughed and Michael smiled. They drove on home and loaded his computer, some towels and bedclothes and dishes and enough cookware to get by. Doug innocently reminded Dee of the mirror just as they were ready to pull away. Michael backed his truck up on their driveway. Doug raced ahead, pulled out his key-chain and unlocked the door in a self-important way that made Dee smile.

'I'm hungry,' said Doug on the way inside.

'We'll get a sandwich as soon as we drop the mirror by your Mom's shop,' said Michael.

'At McDonalds?' asked Doug hopefully.

'Sure, if that's okay with Dee.'

'Fine by me. Doug, grab a banana to hold you over,' suggested Dee. Doug detoured to the kitchen.

The floor on Alice's side of the room was littered in outfits peeled off and left inside out like discarded snake skins. Leaving no room for doubt, Dee indicated with a sweep of her hand her sister's unmade bed and cluttered dresses. 'Alice's side.'

Michael grinned. 'I figured that out.'

Dee saw his gaze skip to her side of the room. She'd dried the rose saved from graduation night and arranged it on her heavy oaken chest of drawers alongside a pair of lacy white gloves, a beaded bag from the twenties and a strand of old pearls. Or was it Doug's rose bowl that'd caught his attention? There wasn't much left of the corsage. The water'd turned black and something that looked suspiciously like mould was floating on top.

'Doug's growing penicillin.' She nudged the wicker basket out of her way, rolled the mirror toward the door and he was still looking at the long-stem rose. Wondering why she'd kept it, no doubt. 'You want to help me here?' she tried to distract him.

Michael sized up the door frame. 'It's not going to go through. We'll have to turn it up on its side.'

Dee had forgotten how heavy the piece was. 'Dad took the mirror off the frame when he brought it in. It's just a couple of screws. I'll be right back.' She hurried off to the basement to get a screw driver.

When Dee came back, her heart nearly stopped, for there stood Michael, her journal in hand. 'Hey!'

He snapped it closed and dropped it back in the basket on the floor while Dee scanned her memory bank in a blind frenzy. The potential for humiliation seemed considerable. But she'd been gone only a minute or two. Could be, in that short length of time, he hadn't seen anything enlightening. Opting for damage control, she said, 'This isn't a library, McKinsey.'

Flustered, red-faced, he stammered, 'Dee, I'm sorry. I just browsed through the basket and. . ..'

'You're lucky Alice didn't catch you.'

'Alice?' His jaw dropped. 'I thought. . .'

'You thought wrong. If it'd been mine, I'd shish-ka-bob you on this screwdriver.' Dee poked him with the screwdriver handle, adding, 'Here, take it. I'll hold the mirror part. And be careful. Mom'll kill us both if we break it.'

Nothing more was said about the journal, but the silence was as thick as the peanut butter Doug'd lathered on his banana. Together, they got the mirror out of the bedroom and safely loaded on to the truck. Dee went back for a quilt and wrapped it around the mirror.

'I'll ride back here just to make sure nothing gets broken,' she said.

'Are you sure?'

She lifted her chin and nodded. He opened his

mouth as if to say something further, then changed his mind, closed the tailgate, circled to the driver's side and got in with Doug. He drove slowly, dodging the pot holes and bumps on the way to her mother's shop. Dee could see Doug through the back window of the truck cab, licking peanut butter off his fingers, pulling the old watch from his pocket, exploring the broken face as he talked. Michael's gaze crossed hers in the rear-view mirror, then darted away.

What had he read? Did he know the notebook was hers? The hot breeze tightened Dee's skin and dried her eyes, minor discomforts compared to nerves jerking around like sweets in a taffy pull. Mixed in with indignation and anxiety was a sense of betrayal. Just a short while ago, she'd been feeling so sorry for him over his grandpa. Dee swept her hand through her hair, trying to shake off the whole scene as Michael parallel-parked in front of the store. He jumped out and came round.

'All in one piece?'

'Seems to be,' said Dee. He offered a hand, but she ignored it and jumped down unassisted.

Doug waited in the truck while they unloaded, reassembled, and moved the mirror into position on the display floor. Dee's mother thanked Michael warmly.

'Glad to help.' Michael crossed to the door and glanced back at Dee. 'Ready for some lunch?'

'I'm going to stick around and help Mom a while.'

'Oh, go on, Dee,' urged Mom. 'It's been slow all morning.'

Dee picked up the feather duster. 'I'm not hungry, okay?'

Michael's ears turned red. He glanced at her mom and shifted uncomfortably. 'You sure you won't come?'

'No thanks. Send Doug in.'

'I already promised him a happy meal at McDonalds. If that's okay.' His gaze skipped to Mom again.

'Micky D's?' chimed Alice from behind the counter. She peeled off her shop apron. 'I suddenly have a craving for a McSimmon.'

'No one invited you, Alice,' said her mother.

'Michael doesn't care, do you, Michael?' prompted Alice, so smoothly it set Dee's teeth on edge.

What could he say? Alice headed for the door, gabbing away about Yolanda and Sally's brother Carl having just landed a job at the land of golden arches. The strap of cow-bells jingled as they closed the door behind them, then all was quiet. Dee dug her nails out of her palms, but her jaw felt like it was out of joint.

'What was that all about?' asked Mom quietly.

Dee carefully righted a stack of old postcards. 'We had a difference of opinion.'

'You want to talk about it?'

'I think I'll go home and throw all of Alice's stuff down in the basement instead. The little troll should be right at home in a subterranean environment.'

'Dee, it isn't Alice's fault you and Michael had a misunderstanding,' reasoned her mother.

'Well, she didn't have to leap at the chance to go with him, now did she?' Blinking back stupid tears, she turned to the door. 'I'm going home.'

'What about Doug?' Mom called after her.

'That's Michael's problem.'

It took Dee forty-five minutes to walk home. She went straight to her room and took out her journal. There were a few recipes on the opening pages and a couple of poems interspersed throughout. Judging by Michael's reaction, though, he hadn't been reading a recipe. He'd looked way too guilty for that. Dee skimmed the more recent entries. Not once had she come right out and said she had a thing for him. But she'd wondered and worried over him quite a bit, using his name over two dozen times in just a few pages.

Hot, sticky, and out of sorts, Dee took Pru's diary from her desk drawer, and skipped back through the entries she'd already read.

'Mr Quinnell buried his wife and newborn child today. He engraved their names on the cradle, and left it to mark the grave site. I looked back as we walked away from the grave and saw the wind, like an unseen hand, gently rocking the cradle. I hadn't known Mrs Quinnell very well, but the sight moved me to tears. Mother too. She held me close and stroked my hair, just as she does the little ones

*when they run to her for comfort. I noticed how
thin she has become and my heart bumped along
like a scared rabbit. I clung to her a long time,
weeping, though not for Mrs Quinnell. Mother was
very patient as if she knew what I myself didn't
quite understand.'*

Reading Pru's words made Dee's own entries
seem so trivial. She wasn't making history like
Prudence, trekking across the continent in search
of a bright new life. Nothing she'd written was
important or riveting enough to catch the imagination of a daughter, granddaughter or great-grand-
daughter years and years from now. Feeling stupid
over the whole thing, Dee ripped a handful of
pages from the spiral binding, wadded them up
and flung them across the room. Just where they
belonged, over there with Alice's mess. Taking
Pru's diary with her, she curled up in the window
seat and thumbed to a more cheerful entry.

*'Seth Hickman rode back to camp on an Indian
pony. He said they'd offered him a wife as a reward
for his brave deed, but he made them to understand he had other prospects, and so they gave him
the pony instead. He looked at me when he said it.
Remembering Fort Kearney and that cocky wink, I
lobbed the head off the goose Father'd shot for dinner and remarked to my little sister Molly, "An
Indian maiden is spared." Father scolded me later
for being impertinent. But Mother patted my arm
and said, "Leave her be."*

Two pages preceding the passage were missing,

so Dee had no way of knowing what Seth Hickman's brave deed had been. Still, she smiled at Pru's spirit, treasuring the glimpses into Pru's heart that breathed life into the tattered diary. Repenting of her tantrum, she retrieved her journal pages, smoothed them out and poked them back inside the spiral notebook. Taking out her pen, she made a fresh entry:

You think you know a guy, but leave him alone in your room a minute and see what happens. Michael 'The Meddler' McKinsey let his fingers do the walking right through my journal! I am so embarrassed, I could die!'

But at the same time, there was a voice in her head, going, 'Get over it! You'd do the same thing if he'd left his private thoughts where you could invade them.' Dee frowned, unhappy with that mocking voice and its defense of Michael. He hadn't diminished her by disrespecting her privacy, he'd diminished himself. So why should she whitewash his flaws? Wearing her feelings like spines on a desert cactus, she wrote in bold letters: 'Michael has always been private about his feelings. That makes what he did all the more indefensible. So nuts to you, Michael. A Mayfield maiden is spared.'

Chapter 11

'MICHAEL'S avoiding ME! He stays inside with his grandpa all day, then leaves the minute his mom gets home from work and doesn't return until late. I bet he's seeing Cheryl again.'

Michael wolfed down his sandwich without tasting it. He couldn't remember a word Alice or Doug had said, yet nearly every word in that single passage from Dee's journal was burned into his brain. It was just a plain notebook. He had no idea it was a journal when he picked it up. Then he opened it and his name jumped out at him. He should have dropped it right then, but of course, he just had to know what she'd said, what she thought, if she felt what he felt. *I blew it big time!*

He hadn't even known Dee had been aware of Cheryl. Or that she'd noticed he'd dodged her after that date/undate fiasco. Her ruse was quick and clever, but he knew her handwriting. He'd hurt her feelings, wounded her trust and made a total ass of himself. And here, just a couple of hours ago, he'd been raving over all the junk in his life over which he had no control. He'd *caused* this. Every bit of it!

Alice's laughter brought him out of his reverie. She was at the counter, teasing Carl Simmons about his mustard yellow power tie. Doug waved to him from a bin of blue balls on the other side of a glass wall. Michael quit beating himself up long enough to return Alice and Doug to their mother at Granny's Attic. He drove to the shop, unloaded his truck and put things away in their temporary home. By mid-afternoon when his mom showed up, he had the apartment in fairly decent order.

'Thanks for pitching in. Once again, you're my hero,' said Mom, taking in all he'd accomplished.

Michael didn't ask about Grandpa or how it had gone, and she didn't volunteer. He could tell by the lines of fatigue, it hadn't been easy. But he kept his guard up, not wanting to feel sorry, for if he once weakened, what he was forced to accept as a temporary remedy could all too easily become Grandpa's permanent home.

Mom followed him back to the house in her own vehicle. They salvaged what little had escaped damage in Grandpa's room and threw away the rest. Bob Findley, Dee's dad, came over to see if they'd heard from the insurance company.

'You're looking at a major repair job. If you've got any remodeling you'd like to do, now would be the time,' he told them.

'I've always wanted a bigger living-room with a fireplace,' Mom admitted. 'A small den would be nice, too.'

Bob clapped Michael on the shoulder. 'This

young man will be leaving the nest one of these days. If you intend staying here indefinitely, you may as well plan according to the changes on the horizon.'

'Where's Grandpa going to sleep?' Michael objected.

'If we move the computer center out of your room into the den, there'd be space for another bed,' Mom reasoned.

His room? Where would he go when he needed some distance?

'Bob's right, you know. We may as well look to the future going into this project,' Mom added. 'After all, how often is the insurance company going to pick up the tab on a remodeling project? What do you think, Michael?'

Afraid he'd jeopardize Grandpa's homecoming if he objected to mom's plan to put Grandpa in his room, Michael said quickly, 'Sure, that'll work.'

Bob listened to Mom's ideas and offered to sketch some floor plans for her approval. At the words 'floor plans' a light went on in Michael's head. Maybe Dee's dad would give him some guidance on his neon shop. He caught himself up short, realizing he was no different from Mom, thinking ahead in terms of remodeling. He was thinking ahead, too. He wrestled with his thoughts, for it seemed callous, somehow, to be looking into the future when Grandpa's problems were so immediate, his future so dismal.

Doug came over. Alice and Dee's mom, too,

shifting his attention back to Dee, who was nowhere to be seen. No doubt about it, he'd trampled her feelings big time. Michael figured the straightest way out of this mess was to be honest about it. He wanted to go over and apologize, even started that way a couple of times only to turn back, worried he'd make matters worse by admitting he knew it was her diary, not Alice's. Then, she'd want to know what he read, and even if he told her, she may have written other things, and worry that he'd read them too. The more he thought, the stickier it got. If only he'd put the thing down the minute he realized what it was!

The electricity at their house still hadn't been restored. At dusk, they drifted out on to the deck. Dee's parents lingered a moment, talking to Mom. Alice started across the grass with Doug at her heels. Michael caught up with them.

'Alice? Tell Dee I'll be working on flags in the morning if she wants to come down to the shop.' He took the easy way out.

'What about me?' asked Doug.

Michael tugged at the bill of Doug's baseball cap. 'We'll find you a job, too.'

'Hear that, Alice? I've got a job now, too.'

'You *are* a job,' Alice retorted.

Doug shot her a shrewd glance. 'I'm going to tell Mom you were holding hands with Yolanda's brother.'

'Liar! Carl took my purse and I was trying to get it back.'

'You could have said "please".'

'He was teasing, doofus.'

'Huh-huh. He was holding your hand.'

Alice was a force to contend with. But Doug was no slouch, sharpening his wits on her as they climbed the deck steps. Spirits lagging, Michael tracked across the yard again and got his neon sign. He wrapped it in a bath towel and took it back to the apartment.

There was no air-conditioning and the bricks were holding on to the day's heat. He was wringing wet by the time he'd hung the neon sign in one of the two windows overlooking the street. He hadn't plugged it in since the 'c' burned out, but he plugged it in now. The gift reminded him of the giver. Would she show up tomorrow to help with the flags? If so, did he put the diary thing behind him and hope she had too? Or did he clear the air? Leaving the sign burning, Michael closed himself in the bathroom, filled Grandpa's old discolored claw-footed tub and wished he could wash the whole problem down the drain.

Mom was home by the time he'd cleaned up. She'd brought a fan for one of the front windows. There was only one bed. Michael left it for his mother and stretched out on Grandpa's old sofa. The stir of air from the fan reached him there, as did the sound of passing cars and the occasional loud laughter of kids passing down on the street.

Mom came out of the bathroom. Guided by the neon sign, she made it to the living-room without turning on a lamp. A chair creaked beneath her. She was in deep shadow, but her bedtime patterns were familiar. Michael followed them with his eyes closed. Dental floss first. One hundred strokes with the hairbrush. Then the lilac-scented moisturizing lotion. The bottle gurgled as she squeezed it.

'You asleep?'

'Not quite.' He shifted on the lumpy sofa.

'I'd forgotten how hot it gets up here. Noisy, too. We've gotten soft, you know it?'

'Guess so.' He lay quietly, drifting on the hum of the fan.

'It should feel like home, but it doesn't.'

'I like it here,' said Michael, for the rich, full memories of this place lay upon him snug as an old quilt. 'Maybe I'll live here some day.'

'You're kidding! It's such a relic. The trudge up those stairs and these flimsy partitions. I can remember when your daddy and I got married how anxious I was to get out of this place. And here I am, back again.' Sounding wistful, Mom added, 'I feel like the hour hand circling a clock. Except that Dad isn't here.'

Her words slowed Michael's thoughts. It occurred to him that since about noon, with the exception of Mom's remodeling plans, he'd worried more about Dee and her diary than he had about Grandpa. And this very minute, Grandpa was bedding down across town in an unfamiliar room with strangers caring for him. Was he feeling bewildered and abandoned? Stomach clenching like a fist, Michael plumped his pillow with unwarranted force.

'He has a room to himself, Michael,' said Mom, as if knowing the path his reflections had taken. 'I stayed for lunch. The food was good and the staff were kind, though overworked, I'm afraid.'

'Were there chairs?'

'Yes.' She didn't elaborate, but he could tell she knew why he'd asked. She gave him space to talk. When he didn't, she filled the silence herself.

'There's an activity room with lots of windows and sunshine. After lunch, some children came from a day care center and sang. One of the mothers who'd come along played the piano. She must have played a dozen hits from the big band days. Dad liked that.'

'Did he dance?'

'No. A few of the patients did, though. There was a girl there, a volunteer. She danced with an old gentleman who would have fit under her arm. It was sweet.'

Michael winced. Sweet was a word for sugar and children and girls like Dee. But not old people. Their childlikeness seemed cruel. 'They give up everything. It's like their lives were for nothing.' He tried to put words to the weight within.

'It's difficult, isn't it? In fact, I wonder at times if it isn't harder on us than it is on Dad.'

Amazed she could think that, Michael rose up on one elbow and said harshly, 'What could possibly be harder than losing your marbles?'

'Counting what you've lost.' Her ankle popped as she got out of the chair. She wished him good night, patted his feet in passing and padded off to bed, trailing the scent of lilacs.

She was partially right, he supposed. This morning, Grandpa had no memory of yesterday's storm. When he fretted, you could distract him. And when he got agitated, you could lead him to memories that calmed. But just because the burdens that had been his for a lifetime had gradually been shifted to sturdier shoulders didn't mean he wasn't suffering. The vacantness in his eyes. The lostness. The awful, awful lostness. Michael kneaded the tight muscles at the base of his neck.

'I almost forgot to tell you,' said his mother from the other side of the partition. 'The girl who danced with the old fellow? Lily? Iris? Rose? Something like that. Anyway, she said she went to school with you.'

'Tulip?'

'Yes, that's it. You know her?'

'Everyone knows Tulip,' said Michael, thinking orange.

'She marches to a different beat, doesn't she?'

Give Mom her dues, she had a gift for tact.

Dee sat in the window-seat, waiting for Sally. She'd just started another letter to Georgia when Sally'd called to say she'd gotten off early and she'd drop by and pick her up if she wanted to spend the night. Dee jumped at the chance. She was packing an overnight case when Alice came in from being next door.

'Michael said to tell you he'll be fixing flags tomorrow, if you want to come down to the shop.' Watching Dee closely, Alice added, 'He told Doug he could help.'

'I hope he and Doug have a good time, then.'

Alice shoved a pile of clean clothes off her bed, grabbed a bottle of nail-polish remover and a cotton wad and sat down. 'Does that mean you're not going?'

'What's it sound like?' Dee kept her face blank.

'What's with you two, anyway? Michael didn't say three words the whole time we were at McDonalds, and he wasn't much more talkative tonight.'

'Makes you wonder. . .is he deep, or just boring?'

'What's deep is your feelings. He likes you, too.' Alice grinned provokingly. 'I'd be miserable, too, with taste like that.'

Dee zipped her overnight bag closed in lieu of a reply and grabbed her purse.

'Where're you going?'

'Sally's house.'

'You're spending the night?' At Dee's nod, Alice put the cap back on the nail-polish remover and grabbed the phone. 'I'm calling Yolanda. Maybe she'll invite me, too.'

'Alice, what would be the point in my going if you're coming too?'

'Well, excuse ME!'

Alice let go of the phone and turned away, but not before Dee saw the quick flash of hurt. She deserved a dose of her own medicine, Dee thought, fortifying herself against fleeting guilt. Teasing Doug all the time. Calling him 'doofus' and 'dweeb'. And going to lunch with Michael.

She turned in the door and said, 'Tell Mom where I went, okay?'

'Tell her yourself.' Alice gave a haughty sniff.

Dee went out on the porch to wait for Sally. She saw Michael's truck next door. A moment later, he came out of the dark house. It would have been easy to call to him. Instead, she watched from porch shadows as he put something on the passenger's seat, circled to the driver's side and drove away.

Dee's parents came home just as Sally arrived. Dee called out a hurried explanation, then jumped into the car. Sally craned her neck, ogling by street light the damage next door.

'That tree sure did a number on Michael's house, huh?'

Dee nodded agreement. 'They spent the night at our house.' She dropped her bag over the seat of Sally's brother's car, and asked, 'How come Carl's trusting you with his car?'

'I led him to believe Alice might be persuaded to come with you.' A wily grin on her face, Sally added as she pulled away from the curb. 'Unfortunately, Alice wasn't home, was she?'

156

'She's home, though not by choice.' Puzzled, Dee backtracked to ask, 'Why would Carl want Alice to come?'

Sally rolled her eyes. 'Get an idea, Dee.'

'You mean. . .Carl and *Alice*?' Incredulous, Dee demanded, 'Since when?'

'Since lately. You really didn't know? Where've *you* been?'

'Preoccupied, apparently.' Dee swept her hair back from her face, Alice's eagerness to do lunch at McDonalds suddenly making more sense. Kind of a gap in ages between her and Carl. Though no more so than Alice and Michael. And wasn't that, in all honesty, at the basis of her annoyance with Alice and the lunch thing? Dee squirmed, uncomfortably aware the more Alice blossomed, the wider the breach between them. 'She was going to call Yolanda once she found out I was spending the night at your house, but I talked her out of it.'

'Wouldn't have done her any good,' said Sally. 'Yolanda and I have made a pact not to get involved in Carl's love life.'

'I'm with you,' said Dee, for in the Simmons family, blood was definitely thicker than water. If the Alice/Carl thing exploded in their faces, she didn't want her friendship with Sally turning up on the casualty list. Besides, Carl fancied himself a real ladies' man, and Alice was only thirteen.

'So where's Michael's family spending the night tonight?' Sally asked, as they tooled toward the downtown business district.

'Over his grandfather's shop. Turn here and we'll cruise by.' Instantly, Dee regretted the impulse. Pru would have more strength of character. 'Or maybe not,' she added hastily.

'Hey, I'm in no hurry,' said Sally, misunderstanding. 'You wanna drop by and get the grand tour?'

'How about we throw rocks instead?'

The light of the instrument panel illuminated Sally's uplifted brow. 'Don't tell me McKinsey has been a jerk again?'

'Worse than a jerk, he read my journal,' Dee blurted.

Sally's eyes widened. 'You're kidding! Where'd he find it?'

'The wicker basket.'

'In your bedroom?' Sally grinned wickedly. 'Seems to me there's some gaps in this story.'

'We were taking my mirror down to the Attic.'

'Down to the attic? The story gets stranger and stranger,' Sally teased. 'Are you sure you aren't hiding something from me?'

'Granny's Attic. You know what I mean! Anyway, I went to get a screwdriver.'

'That's when he got nosy?'

Dee nodded. Already, she regretted her letter to Georgia. She sure wasn't going to make a confession to Sally too.

'Wasn't anything in there about me, was there? Anything personal, I mean?'

'No! And thanks a lot for your concern,' Dee said testily.

Sally had the grace to looked ashamed. 'I'm sorry, Dee. Really. I'll stop and you can throw a rock. Just don't break anything, okay?'

Dee sighed. 'I better pass. In our family, it's okay to get your name in the paper, just so long as it isn't in the court notes.'

Sally grinned. Bugs swarmed in the beam of their headlights as she stopped for a red light. She shot Dee a curious glance. 'So what did he read?'

'I don't know. He snapped it shut when I came in. I didn't want to show undue interest. Not after I'd told him it was Alice's journal.'

'That's rich.'

'Except he may know my handwriting.'

Sally reached across the seat and patted her arm. 'Shake it off, Dee. You guys have been friends for so long, chances are McKinsey knows all your secrets anyway.'

Not hardly. Dee swept her hand through her hair as Sally slowed for Mr Kolupa's block. She lifted her gaze as they passed the old tailor shop. The green neon sign she'd given Michael lit the second-storey window. She saw with a pang that the 'c' had burned out. *Fitting. A flawed mirror reflecting a fractured relationship.*

Chapter 12

'We drove by Mr Kolupa's old shop on the way to Sally's house last night. The neon sign I gave Michael for graduation was hanging in the window. One letter has burned out, a visual reminder of how things have burned out between Michael and me. Bummer!

Sally's still in the dark over my true feelings for Michael. (I know I said 'Nuts to Michael!' And I even started a letter to Georgia to retract what I said before. But my heart keeps saying maybe there's a way to get beyond this.) Listen to me! I'm like Doug, forever wanting to fix broken things! Speaking of which – you know what he wants to do? He wants to take that old watch to the jeweler down town to be fixed. I told him he could probably buy a new one cheaper. But he looked so disappointed, I felt mean.

Anyway, back to Michael. He told Alice last evening to tell me he'd be working on flags today, if I wanted to come down to the shop. Truth is, I'd like to help with the flags. It'd be a real job. And it'd be neat, establishing our own business. Setting our own hours. Doing our own thing. But I don't know what he read or what he's thinking or how to act. I'm still feeing embarrassed, maybe more embarrassed than mad, even. You know, it was a lot easier when I thought of him as just a friend! Enough already, I'm boring myself!

Sally's got the coolest family. Last night we were all sitting out on the deck talking and I found out that her mom and dad met at a rock festival and had known one another only six weeks when they got married. Can you believe it? They were reminiscing and playing old records and looking through picture albums and it hit me. Back then, they were just having a good time, not thinking at all about being a tiny piece of history. Just like Pru and her diary. Does that mean we all are, in our own way, making history day by day? What an awesome thought! I wish I could think of something important to write – something that will stand out a hundred years from now.

But since I can't. . .more about the sleep-over at Sally's. We came inside about midnight, and spent what was left of the night watching a movie we'd rented from the video shop, playing CDs and talking. Seemed like I'd just closed my eyes when Mom was there to take me home so I could watch Doug. He's getting bored with my lazing around. Maybe we'll catch the bus and go downtown.'

Dee put her journal away, then spent a few minutes in front of the bathroom mirror trying to repair the damage of too little sleep. She wasn't planning on stopping by Michael's. But downtown, you just never knew who you might bump into.

'Doug? Change your shirt and we'll go to the shop. Maybe Mom'll spring for lunch,' Dee called as she exited the bathroom.

Doug materialized at her elbow. 'Can we eat at McDonalds?'

'You just ate there yesterday. How about the tea-room instead?'

'Cucumber sandwiches. Yuk!' Doug wrinkled his nose.

Dee sighed, too tired to point out there were other things on the menu. 'Okay, okay. Mcdonalds it is. If Mom'll let us use the car,' she added quickly, for the fast-food restaurant wasn't on the bus route and she didn't want to walk that far. She gathered her sunglasses on the way and was about to lock the front door when a familiar pickup truck pulled into the drive.

'Michael!' Doug broke into a gap-toothed smile and raced down the drive.

'Hi, bud.'

Dee felt Michael's glance skip from her to Doug and back again. Her heart bumped against her ribcage. She caught a shallow breath, ill at ease as he draped an arm over Doug's shoulder.

'How's it going, Dee?'

'Okay. You?' she returned stiffly.

'Okay, I guess.' He tipped his ball cap to the back of his head. 'I've got a whole stack of flags waiting. Thought maybe you needed a ride.'

'Ride where?'

'To the shop. Didn't Alice give you my message?'

Dee tightened her grip on her keys and hid behind her sunglasses, trying to figure him out. *Did he really think she was on her way to the shop? Or was that just his way of sweeping the whole deal under the rug?*

'We were going to take the bus,' Doug filled the silence. He added in a rush, 'But I'll ride with you if you want. Okay, Dee?'

'Run back inside and get your watch,' Dee avoided a direct answer.

'But you said. . .'

'Get it and we'll stop by the jewelers. There's no harm in asking for an estimate.' Dee reversed her earlier decision, partly to make him happy, partly to steal a moment alone with Michael.

Doug broke into a delighted smile and trotted back inside.

Michael stopped on the bottom step, close enough she noticed the dark smudges beneath his blue eyes. 'Where were you headed, *really*?' he asked.

Dee stuck out her her chin. 'The jewelers, lunch, Granny's Attic. Not necessarily in that order.'

'Were you stopping by the shop?'

'I wasn't planning on it.' She swatted a mosquito and flicked it off her arm.

'Thought you were going to help with the flags.'

'That was before. . .'

Michael shifted his weight, looking every bit as uncomfortable as she felt, and a good deal more contrite. 'I didn't know it was your diary when I started reading, Dee,' he came clean. 'Once I realized, I could've stopped, but I didn't because I saw my name and I was curious. I'm really sorry.'

'Forget it. What's done is done.' She averted her gaze, so embarrassed she wished the earth would make like giant jaws and swallow her whole. 'I better see what's keeping Doug.'

Michael bounded up the steps and between her and the door. 'Just hear me out. Please?'

'Okay, okay, since you're dying to tell me – what'd you read?'

'I'm not dying to tell you, I want to clear the air, that's all,' said Michael. 'It was pretty brief. Something about me avoiding you.'

Dee braced herself for more. 'And?'

'That was about it. You were right too. I was avoiding you. But only because things weren't going well with Grandpa and I figured if you got too close, you'd realize how bad he was and somehow, I thought I was protecting him. No, that's not it yet,' he amended, shaking his head.

'Too close?' echoed Dee. Her pulse beat at her temples and her throat went dry. A deep stain rushed up his neck, making her even more uncomfortable. 'Never mind, just let it go.'

'No, I can't. Not until it's settled.' He stuffed the tips of his fingers into jean pockets and thrust out his jaw. 'Truth is, sometimes Grandpa is hard to take. I was protecting myself from what you might think.'

'You should know better!' she blurted.

'Than to read your diary? It was wrong and I'm sorry.'

'I mean, you should know better than to worry what I'd think about your grandpa.'

He shifted uneasily. 'We get some real odd looks. After so much of that. . .'

Heart melting, she asked, 'When did I ever give you an odd look?'

'You're giving me one now.'

'Am I? Maybe I am,' she conceded, just wanting this over and done with now and on to something less excruciating. 'But it has nothing to do with your grandfather.'

'What, then?'

'Since when, I'd like to know, am I the kind to ditch a friend just because someone in his family is a little eccentric?'

'Grandpa isn't eccentric, he's sick,' Michael said bluntly. 'Alzheimer's isn't like cancer or a heart condition. On the surface, he looks okay. So a lot of people don't understand. They either ignore him, or treat him like a kid who's acting up for attention. If you try to tell them, they get uncomfortable and say stuff like 'He could do better if he'd try.' Or 'He's just a little forgetful.' Or, 'He's having a bad day, that's all.' It's easier just not to talk about it.'

'Okay, if that's how you feel. We won't talk about it,' said Dee, meaning it.

Looking doubtful, he asked, 'Would you come to the shop? Just for a second. It's nothing to do with the flags.'

Doug came back out of the door before Dee could answer. He turned his face up, looking from Dee to Michael and back again. 'Are we taking the bus?'

'No. Michael's giving us a lift.' Dee took the steps down, motioned Doug into the middle seat, and climbed into the truck after him. She was glad he was there as a buffer, for she'd never felt more awkward in her life. Had she melted down too easily? Was she, in her eagerness to patch this up and be with him, avoiding a larger issue? She still didn't know for sure what he'd read – more than he was saying, she was sure. She didn't want him to think he could tramp over her in combat boots without her letting out a peep.

'Dee stayed the night with Sally last night,' said Doug, interrupting her thoughts.

Michael looked past him and ventured, 'So what'd you do?'

Drove by your place. Felt rotten because the way things were between us. Realizing just how bad she had it for him, Dee felt suddenly unnerved. She touched Doug's arm and asked, 'Have you got your watch? Good. Drop us here is fine, Michael.'

Looking disappointed, Michael pulled over to

the curb in front of the jewelry store. He asked, 'Are you going to stop by the shop?'

'Maybe. I guess. In a bit.' Heat rushed to her face. She pushed her pocketbook strap high on her shoulder and held the door for Doug. *I'm not good at these games*, she thought, as he pulled away. And yet she couldn't let herself fall all over him. But what good was it, trying to hold on to her anger? Like she was trying to punish him, or something. He'd said he was sorry. He couldn't un-read what he'd read. They had to get it settled, not the journal. As far as she was concerned, that was over and done. What was between them. Or wasn't between them. That's what needed settling. It was making her crazy. Picking up vibes. Sensing, but not being sure.

Doug benefited from her rattled state. She left the watch at the shop to be fixed, even though it would indeed cost more to fix than to replace. They got the car from Mom and did the lunch thing at Mickey D's, with Alice tagging along. By the time Dee returned Mom's car, Doug and Alice to the shop, an hour had elapsed. Promising Mom she'd be back for Doug in a while, she walked the two blocks to Michael's.

The shop was unlocked. Light streamed through the plate glass window, showing off the nicks and bumps and blemishes of the old building. Michael's computer looked out of its era, sitting on the old scarred counter. The cursor blinked from the lighted screen, but there was no sign of Michael.

'Michael?' Dee circled the counter and paused in the doorway that led into the back room. 'Where are you?'

'Upstairs.'

Dee backtracked and looked up through the grate. All she could see was the bottom of his shoes. But his voice carried well through the grate as he added, 'Can I bring you a soda?'

'Nothing for me.' She heard him pull the tab on a can.

'I put together a more efficient work space in the back for the flag mending. I went ahead and set up my computer, too. Figured we could use it to keep track of our accounts. You know, for billing purposes,' he filled her in, still moving around a floor above. 'I picked up a bunch of flags this morning. Guess I'll get down to business this afternoon.'

Getting a crick in her neck from peering up through the grate, Dee said, 'Come downstairs, would you? I told Mom I'd be back shortly.'

'Be right there.'

Legs aching from too little sleep, Dee dropped into the only chair in the room. It faced his computer. Her bleary eyes scanned the screen. All at once, she leaned closer.

'Grandpa called me 'Richard' again,' the entry read, *'Just my luck he'd say it in front of Dee. It pushed her pity button, I could tell. Too bad I'm not looking for sympathy.'*

What on earth? Hearing Michael's footsteps behind her, Dee swung around in the chair. She gestured toward the screen, blurting, 'What's this?'

'What's it look like?'

Heat swept up her neck. But before guilt could get her in a stranglehold, she said, 'You keep a journal? How come you never mentioned it before?'

'There's a lot of things I haven't mentioned.'

'But you left it right here on the screen!' she protested. 'If you didn't want me to read it. . .'

'I wanted you to read it,' he said, surprising her. 'It was the only way I knew of squaring things up. And of explaining. . .'

'This isn't the same thing,' she objected, suddenly getting the picture. 'This is hand picked. I mean, if I was going to browse, say like this. . .' She weighed him with a glance. 'Let's see. Which key? Arrow, maybe.' A pink-tipped finger poised over the keyboard, she looked to the screen and back at him again.

He was one stride from being between her and the keyboard. Seeming to struggle with himself, he shoved his hands in his pockets in such a way she got the feeling he put them there to keep from reaching around her and shutting down the whole works. It really was his journal! He hadn't just typed those words to square things up.

'Open apple, up arrow. Just promise not to sell it to the *Inquire*,' he added with obvious discomfort.

Dee left her hands drift to her lap. She reread the entry he'd left on the screen and said with more pluck than truthfulness. 'You're wrong about me. I don't have any pity buttons.'

'I'm starting to realize. . .' he began, moisture beading his brow.

'You're wrong about the sympathy thing, too,' she added for good measure.

'Okay.'

Screwing up all her courage, she angled him a hooded glance and asked, 'So what is it you're looking for?'

His ears turned red. But he held her gaze. 'A chance to know you in a different way. Not just as friends. That's why I chose this entry,' he added, gesturing toward the screen. 'So you'd see how it is. I wanted to tell you. But you've got a look about you that intimidates the heck out of me.'

'Really?' She couldn't hold back a smile.

'So what do you think?' he challenged quietly.

'About what?'

'About us?'

His words dropped into a chasm of silence. Finger tracing a groove in the counter, she sneaked a glance and said finally, 'Are we really having this conversation? It's awfully awkward, isn't it?'

'Only because we've been friends for so long and it's hard to start thinking in other terms. We can give it a shot, though. If you want to, that is.'

'I think I'd like that,' she murmured.

There was relief in every curve of his smile. He reached for her hand. 'Come on into the back, and I'll give you the grand tour.'

Dee's pounding heart settled into a safer rhythm as Michael led her into the back room and showed her the set-up. Pins, scissors, marking pencils and a T-square were arranged at one end of a long table. Just beyond the table was a heavy-duty sewing-machine with a good light hanging over it. There was a shelving unit too, still smelling of dusting polish. The flags on both shelves had identification tags pinned to them.

'Flags in, flags out.' Michael indicated one shelf, then the other.

'Better than I expected, from a guy who chooses open grates over dustpans.'

'I figured I'd better do it right, or you'd want to be boss.'

She wagged her head. 'You've mistaken me for Alice.'

He grinned. 'If it means you're going to let me be the boss, then I guess I'll be gutsy and ask when do you want to start?'

'How about right now?' said Dee.

'I thought your Mom was expecting you back.'

'I'll call her and tell her to send Doug this way when he gets bored,' said Dee.

'Park your pocketbook up there on the shelf, then.'

Dee did so, then stood by watching as Michael used the T-square to mark a cutting line, then grabbed the scissors and cut off the ragged end. Next, he turned the rough edges under twice, secured it with pins and sat down at the machine.

He had to slow for the heavy seams where red and white stripes met. The whole process took about fifteen minutes.

'You want to cut or sew?' he asked, when he'd finished.

Insecure with her sewing capabilities, Dee chose cutting and pinning. There were a couple of company flags and some state flags, too, but the majority were American flags. Some, she soon realized, couldn't be salvaged, for if cut back too far the striped part was out of proportion to the field of blue. Gradually, she became more adept and the system went fairly smoothly.

About mid afternoon, Alice and Doug came into the shop. Alice showed herself around, then left. But Doug stayed. Michael put him in charge of gathering up scraps and folding finished flags. Time passed quickly. By five o'clock, when Mom and Alice stopped to pick them up, they'd finished a dozen flags.

'Better hurry, Mom's double-parked,' Alice warned.

'Go on, Dee. I'll sweep up,' urged Michael. His hands brushed hers as he took the broom.

The prickle of awareness along her nerve endings was an instant reminder of the shift in their relationship. Once again, she felt excited and awkward and gauche all at once. She grabbed her pocketbook and hurried after Alice and Doug. But Michael followed her to the curb.

'Thought I'd deliver the flags around town after

173

dinner. Do you want to come along?' he invited.

'Sure.' Aware of Alice hanging her ear out the car window, Dee asked, 'What time?'

'How about seven?'

'Fine by me. See you then.'

Alice swept Michael a curious look. 'Are you two going out?' she asked as Dee climbed into the back seat.

'Flag run, Al. Don't get excited,' said Dee, hugging her secret close. She snapped her seat-belt and worked hard at keeping her face blank. Her shoulders ached from leaning over the table all afternoon. But her heart sang all the way home.

Dee showered after dinner and dressed in stone-washed jeans and a short denim shirt that resembled a denim jacket with the sleeves cut out. A gold chain, gold loop earrings and a gold bracelet softened the outfit. She curled her hair loosely about her shoulders and was on the porch waiting when Michael pulled into the driveway at seven.

They made stops all over town, running twelve flags up twelve poles. The mild summer evening was dwindling down to a purple twilight as they stopped by Truckers' Plaza for soft drinks. Sally was bearing down on them as Michael slid into the booth, facing Dee across the table.

'Little ice to go with those Cokes?' Sally asked, when they ordered.

'Yeah. We'll take glasses, too,' Michael played along.

Dee smiled, for this evening he seemed more

like the old Michael, the relaxed easy-going next-door-neighbour guy, with one obvious difference: there was chemistry between them now that made her pulse race.

Sally looked past him and asked Dee with a dead-pan expression, 'So, what're you doing running around with this clown?'

'We're in business together. Tell her, Michael.'

'Oh, so it was a *business* dispute!' Sally grinned boldly and whispered behind her hand, 'She wanted to rock your window last night, McKinsey. But I wouldn't let her. Keep that in mind when you put down a tip.'

'Get us a real waitress, then we'll talk,' said Michael.

Ignoring Dee's protests over the rock thing, Sally swatted Michael's shoulder with her tablet and turned away. When she came back with their Cokes, Tulip was right on her heels. Her jeans were wrinkled and the fringe on her western shirt looked as if it skimmed most of the plates she'd served that day.

She gave them both a wave, but honed right in on Michael. 'I met your grandfather today, Mike.'

'Mr Kolupa? Where?' asked Dee, though Michael said nothing.

'He ate lunch at Mr Oppenheimer's table.'

'That's her boyfriend,' Sally inserted, eyes twinkling.

'Mr Oppenheimer? The old guy in front of the building downtown?' said Dee as the name

175

dropped into place. The age gap was too strange, even for Tulip. 'Who is he, really?'

'It's hard to define who a person is, don't you think?' Tulip philosophized. 'Mr Oppie's son, a father, a grandfather and a great-grandfather. Oh, and he was a night watchman for a little farming community for about a hundred years.'

'He's a resident at the Rosewood. Tulip helps out there,' Sally cleared up the mystery.

'So what'd you do, take him on an outing?' asked Dee, then added at Tulip's nod, 'That's cool. Did he get his wallet back?'

'There was no wallet. But then, there were no hooligans either. Mr Oppie frets needlessly some-times.'

'Then why. . .' Dee paused and glanced at Michael. He hadn't said a word since Tulip had mentioned his grandfather.

Tulip's attention shifted to him as well. She pat-ted him on the head in much the same affectionate way Dee often patted Doug. 'I'll be seeing you at the home, Mikey.'

She gave them both a little wave and clumped off in her cowboy boots, missing Michael's soft-spoke, 'Don't count on it.'

Chapter 13

'As we walked out to the truck at the Plaza, Michael held the door for me on the driver's side. A clear invitation to stay close, Dee penned in her journal. 'The gear shift was on the floor, so I had to angle my knees out of the way every time he shifted gears. My thoughts kept shifting, too. Had Sally caught on there was something more than business going on between Michael and me? I ought to wring her neck for telling him about that rock thing! What about Tulip, patting Michael on the head? She wasn't flirting, Tulip doesn't do flirting. It was more like empathizing. Over his grandpa, I guess. Maybe she sees a lot of folks like him, working at a nursing home. Two jobs! Michael's 'Don't count on it' kept echoing too. He surely didn't mean to say he has no plans to visit his grandpa. I wanted to ask him as we drove home. But I admit it, my main shift in attention kept grinding home to that "Is this date going to end in a kiss?" gear. He's so private on the subject of his grandfather, I didn't want to rock the boat by asking questions. Michael may have been thinking about some of the same *things I was. The closer we got to my house, the deeper the silence. Neither one of us realized until later that Paula was inside with my folks – that would've really killed the mood. Luckily, she'd parked in the driveway next door, and it was so dark, neither of us noticed her car sitting there. Anyway, to make a short story long, Michael smiled as he walked me to the door and said, 'You make things fun, Dee.' He said it in such a way, I realized he hadn't been having much fun lately. I thought of Pru and how bleak her journal entry when tragedy struck out on the plains of the Nebraska Territory. I've never had to face anything like that tough. But I tried for a second to put myself in her place as she stood by her mother's grave. Or in Michael's, coping with his grandpa's illness. It was as if a stinging wind blew over my soul. Misunderstanding, Michael asked if I was cold. He slipped his arm around me, and the rest, as they say, is history. It occurred to me, though, that maybe there are things in Pru's journal that would be meaningful to Michael. Because of his father. And because of what he's facing with his grandfather.'*

'What're you doing?' Alice asked from across the room.

'Scribbling down some recipes,' Dee fibbed.

'But you're smiling.'

'They're happy recipes.'

Alice punched her pillow and grumbled, 'And you think *I'm* a moron!'

'No I don't. I think you're a troll.'

'Did he kiss you?' her sister asked slyly.

Dee reached over and snapped out the light.

'Did he?'

'Yes, Alice, he did,' said Dee, more secure since that kiss. It felt good to say it. To have it in the open. To revel in the delight of that moment.

Alice was silent a moment, then accused, 'You're lying.'

Dee smiled in the darkness. Nothing could ruin this evening, not even Alice. She closed her eyes, reliving the kiss. At first, she'd yielded more than participated, because when it came right down to the moment, it was awkward, being kissed by a guy who'd been like a brother for so many years. But Michael was a pretty good kisser. She got all fluttery inside, and kissed him back. It stood out as an electric moment, one which promised an interesting future. Her heart was galloping along when the porch light came on. They stepped apart just as the door opened.

Paula's bemused gaze had encompassed them both a moment before she'd explained they'd been working on remodeling drawings and would they like to come inside and take a look? Michael pored over the plans with Dad while Paula and the rest of Dee's family mingled in the living-room, eating popcorn and offering personal opinions on what the remodeling should include. Doug suggested a repair room for broken things, then hid his face against Dad's arm when everyone smiled.

Dee yawned, her eyes growing heavy. Tomorrow was Friday. Dad planned to start building next door on Monday. Michael would be there helping her father all day every day until the job was done. Flags, she guessed, would have to wait until evening. That was a bright prospect too. She hugged her pillow, thinking things might not have worked out nearly so well if she'd gotten that job at the Plaza.

There was demolition needing to be done before the repairs and remodeling could begin on the house. In the interest of keeping to the budget imposed by the insurance company, Dee's father encouraged Michael to tear out the walls that were in the way, thereby saving some labor expense. Michael rolled off Grandpa's mohair sofa bright and early on Friday morning and was on hand when Bob Findley stopped by before leaving for another site. Bob explained what had to come down, gave him instructions, put a sledgehammer in his hands and left him to it.

After the sedentary weeks of keeping watch over Grandpa, Michael tore into the hot, dusty job with a vengeance. It was good to feel muscles gathering force in his arms and shoulders. He relished the impact of hammer hitting home. Even the rain of debris was gratifying. Best of all, the task took enough thought to crowd out all other concerns.

Michael took a break a mid-morning when Dee and Doug showed up with home-made cookies and milk. Blisters were forming on his hands and he'd swallowed enough dust to choke a mule. But he enjoyed the mini-picnic on the ground where the old red maple had stood a short while ago.

When the last morsel was gone, Michael stretched out on the blanket Dee had spread and cradled his head on one arm. Noticing his hands, Dee suggested Doug run inside for some band-aids and a pair of work gloves.

'You don't have to, Doug. I'm fine. Really,' said Michael.

Doug, well on his way, hollered back. 'No you're not. I'll be the doctor, okay?'

Michael squinted at Dee and accused. 'See what you started?'

She broke off a seeded dandelion and teased. 'Too bad the tree's gone. A week ago, he was into dandelion and maple leaf poultices.'

Michael grinned and tugged at the bill of his cap to shade his eyes. 'I kind of miss that old tree.'

'Me, too. Though not for poultices. Pretty grue-some-looking medicine.' Dee gazed at sky the branches used to obliterate and mused, 'It was a nice tree. Remember the tire swing?'

'And the fort your dad built for us? We had to climb the rope to get in.'

'Yes! And in the fall, we used to swing out on that rope, then jump into a pile of leaves.'

'Me Tarzan, you Jane,' he said, grinning.

Dee poked him and protested. 'That isn't the way it was at all. You said it was a swamp and the piles of leaves were a raft, and if I landed anywhere else, the alligators would get me.'

'You've still got all your toes, don't you?'

Dee's laughter dwindled down to a regretful sigh. 'It's kind of sad, you know? All those years to grow and then, zap, it's gone. Left a pretty big hole in the yard, too.' She shot a glance toward the back alley where they'd stacked all the branches too small to be cut into firewood.

'Who'd guess you'd get sentimental over a tree?' said Michael, grinning.

Heat stole up her neck. But she returned his smile and admitted. 'Guess I am, sort of.'

'We can plant another tree once the remodeling is done.'

'Yes,' she sighed. 'But it won't be the same.'

'No,' Michael agreed. He added on a practical note, 'This time, we'll plant something that won't outgrow the house.'

Doug returned with the first-aid kit and gloves, ending the moment alone. Once the doctoring was done, Michael went back to work. But Dee's words about the tree leaving a hole lingered, for they applied to more than just trees. Just last night, watching Doug hanging at his father's elbow as they went over the building plans, he had felt that old twinge of all he had missed. And now it was Grandpa. He was like a gnarly old oak standing alone. The branches bare and broken. The bark peeling away. Green vigor a distant memory. And still, he stood. Tightly lashed emotions jerked at his heart strings. He put all he had into the next swing of the sledgehammer and crowded out the pain.

Mom and the whole Findley tribe helped clean up the debris of demolished walls on Saturday. That night, Michael and Dee repaired the last of the flags he had collected following the storm, then delivered them round on Sunday afternoon. They stopped for pizza afterwards. Dusk found them lingering on her front porch. When the conversation lagged, Dee reached into her pocketbook and pulled out a tattered leather-bound book.

'What've you got there?'

'A diary.'

The rusty chain on the porch swing creaked as he covered his eyes in mock horror. 'Not that again!'

Dee smiled. 'It's not mine. Well, it *is* mine. Mom gave it to me on my birthday. But my great-great-grandmother wrote it. It's her account of traveling west with her family to the Oregon Territory in 1851.'

Impressed, he gave the small book a second look. 'That's quite a keepsake.'

She nodded and slid him a bashful glance. 'I thought maybe you'd like to hear some of it.'

The fact that she'd had the diary in her pocketbook indicated this was more than sudden impulse. What was it she wanted him to hear? He touched the worn leather binding. 'Tell me first, does it have a happy ending?'

183

'I'm not sure, yet,' she admitted. 'I haven't finished it.'

'But your birthday was in April, wasn't it?'

'April the second. That's when Prudence made her first entry. I thought it'd be cool to read it as she wrote it.' Dee opened the fragile book to the first page. 'She didn't write every day. Sometimes, when it was the same old, same old, she didn't write for two, three weeks at a time.'

Michael noted how gently she cradled the small book. 'When's the last entry?'

'September the fifteenth.'

'And you haven't peeked ahead at all? Come on, tell the truth!' he ribbed.

'Not once. Honest.' She uncurled the leg beneath her, and set the swing to swaying. 'This way, I'm sharing the adventure with her. If I knew the outcome, it'd take away from the suspense.'

'Got to hand it to you – you've got self-control. You've also got me curious. Go ahead. Read.'

Michael locked his hands behind his head as she began reading. The first page wasn't all that compelling. A girl, the oldest of six girls, feeling excited and sad and a little scared about trading all that was familiar for the unknown, trusting in her parents' judgement that they could make a better life in the west. But slowly, he felt himself being sucked into her account of folks of different backgrounds traveling together, some becoming fast friends, others causing conflict even more troublesome than broken axles, swollen rivers, bad water, sickness, and Indian encounters. The sun set, the fireflies flitted across the grass and mothers called children indoors. Dee flicked on the porch light, and settled closer to the light. Michael watched her face in the shadows and should have been prepared for Pru's mother's death. But the swift, starkness of it caught his off-guard as Dee's voice dropped almost to a whisper:

"*As I stood by Mother's grave, my sisters weeping and clinging to me like little possums, I knew my life was forever changed. Father says that her spirit has gone home to the One who gave it and that we shall all be reunited some day. He meant the words to comfort. But I'm feeling angry instead that she came all this way only to die. I have no heart for the journey now. It is pointless, the cost too dear. But what is there to do but continue on?*"

The years fell away, the words as fresh as the day they were written. The stricken note, the silent wail. Aware of his pulse throbbing at his temple in the silence that followed, Michael asked, 'That's it?'

Nodding, Dee closed the diary. 'She lost her mother on the third of June. There isn't another entry until the twenty-fourth June.'

'That's a few days yet. Sure you don't want to read ahead?'

'Michael!' she reproved with a small smile.

He slid his arm along the back of the swing, his fingertips brushing her shoulder. 'Okay, okay. Hooks you though, doesn't it?'

'It's sad,' she said simply.

But his thought reached beyond the sorrow. For the journey was far from pointless. Pru and others like her, by continuing on, changed the face of America forever. *It wasn't superhuman courage, it was faithful plodding*. Grandpa, too. For one brief instant, looking back across nearly a century and a half, he understood the human experience on a broader scale. It had not changed. A precious few lived their lives like comets streaking across the heavens. Others, like weeds growing under a stone, grew pale and twisted toward a bitter destiny. But for the vast majority, it was faithful plodding. Vowing to hold on to the thought for the next time he felt like blowing off everyone and everything, he thanked Dee for sharing her prize.

'I'm glad you liked it,' she said with a touch of sadness. 'I was afraid you'd be bored.'

'No, not at all. It's pretty exciting, actually.'

Doug came out and wriggled between them and tested the strength of the chains with his swinging. Eventually, Dee's Mom told him it was his bedtime, and reluctantly he went back inside. A short while later, Michael rose to go as well. He felt as content as he'd been in a while as Dee walked him to his truck, said good-night, and tilted her face to his. It was a lot sweeter when you said it with a kiss.

Monday was good. Tuesday, too, with Bob Findley hard at remodeling. Bob worked like a Trojan and expected no less of him, which suited Michael just fine. He was learning things that would serve him well when it came to building a neon room. They had the house all closed in by Tuesday morning. The lumberyard delivered bricks and a pile of sand on Wednesday. Doug, the collector, turned from gathering blocks and other scrap lumber to playing in the sand.

'All done,' said Dee, finished poking scraps of fiberglass insulation in around the new windows. she pulled off her gloves. 'Have you got another job for me? Preferably something a little less itchy.'

Her father, busy nailing together two by fours for the den wall, paused a moment. 'Sweep up all this sawdust, would you Dee, before Doug thinks of a use for it?'

'Give me a break, Dad. You're either sending me for donuts or shoving a broom in my hands,' Dee complained, scratching both arms.

Michael cajoled, 'But Dee, you're so good with a broom.'

'Or maybe you'd rather do some more insulating,' Bob chimed in. 'Like around the front door.'

'Definitely woman's work,' Michael teased, for he had helped cut and fit blankets of the stuff into the walls, and knew how itchy the fiberglass insulation was.

'You're both living in the dark ages.' Dee faked an injured sniff, and gave the floor such a vigorous sweeping all three of them were coughing by the time she made for the door with a shovel full of sawdust.

'There's a garbage can out back,' her father called after her. He drove another nail with the air-gun, then gestured toward a pile of drywall board, saying to Michael, 'That's piled right where we need to put the other wall. May as well move it, now that she's swept.'

They were half-way across the room with the first piece of sheet rock when Doug let out a terrified shriek. 'Daddy, Daddy! Dee's on fire!'

Dee's dad dropped his end of the drywall board and ran out the front door. Michael let his end down too, tore through the kitchen and out the sliding glass door. He leapt off the deck and covered the backyard on ground-eating strides, racing for the alley and the pile of brush he'd set fire to that morning.

Dee lifted her head and saw him coming. Doubled over, beating back flames licking at her jeans, she squealed, 'Yikes, it's going to burn through!'

Adrenalin rushing, pulse thundering, Michael pushed Dee to the ground. It took only a second to roll out the flames.

'I'm okay. It's out, I'm okay!' She scrambled to her feet as her dad bore down on them.

White-lipped, breathing hard, her father's temper snapped. 'You threw it on the fire, didn't you? I told you the garbage can. Don't you ever listen?'

Cheeks stained, voice shrinking, she said, 'I didn't know it would flame up like that.'

'Of course it flames up. Just like gasoline!'

'Sorry,' she said meekly.

'Sorry doesn't cut it! Go on home. I haven't time for this.' Bob turned away.

An uncomfortable silence followed as Dee's father stalked back to the house. Michael shifted from foot to foot, unable to think of a thing to say to ease Dee's embarrassment. Dee leaned over and dusted her singed jeans.

Doug squatted down in front of her and peered anxiously into her face. 'I can call 9-1-1.'

She straightened and managed a pinched smile. 'Thanks, Dougie. But I'm fine.'

'Your dad was scared, Dee. That's all.' Michael tried to take away the sting of her father's flare-up.

'Don't you think I know that?' Looking injured, she gazed after her father, then turned for home. But not before Michael saw tears gather.

Chapter 14

'I shouldn't have snapped at Michael. It isn't his fault Dad's such a grump. He couldn't just say he was scared. No! he had to act like a big jerk and embarrass me in front of Michael. He can't ever say what he's feeling. Come to think of it, Michael's not very good at it either.'

Dee glanced out the window. Doug was playing on the swing set out back. Apparently, he was avoiding Dad too. Dad's gruffness quelled even Alice. Only Mom seemed immune to it. No, not immune. It was more like she saw through the layers and responded to what he was feeling. Dee grew pensive, remembering how Pru's father had snapped at Pru and her sisters after a grueling day of lowering wagons down a steep canyon. Hard work hadn't sweetened his disposition, either. Wasn't anything to be gained by sulking, though. Not then, and not now.

Dee snapped her journal closed. She'd showered and washed her hair since coming inside. The jeans she'd been wearing had protected her legs, so physically she was not worse for the experience.

But her thoughts itched worse than the fiberglass insulation she'd been poking around the windows earlier. She pitched her journal into the basket, then thought better of it. Alice asking what she was writing the other night warranted more care. Crossing the room, she hid her journal among the litter of teen magazines and old school papers beneath Alice's bed. There were dust balls thicker than drier lint. Seemed like a pretty safe hiding place.

Doug came inside, looking for a playmate. He pulled a shoe-box full of Match Box cars out of his toy box and made orphan eyes at her. 'You want to build roads in the sand?'

It wasn't high on Dee's list of fun, fun, fun. But she was tired of her own company. She agreed on the condition she could be the road commissioner, overseeing from the shade while he built the roads. With the maple tree gone, the only shade near the sand pile was that thrown by the shadow of the house. Grabbing the beach towel Alice had left on the line since Sunday, Dee stretched out and got comfortable while Doug grabbed one of Dad's old hard hats and settled down to road building. Before long, he'd crisscrossed the whole sand pile with roads. He had Match Box cars going every which way. Wiping the sweat out of his eyes, he expanded the sand pile into a village, using as pretend buildings blocks he'd salvaged from Michael's house.

'This is our house. This is the bank. And here's

the school. See the flagpole?' He punched a stick into the sand.

'You can call it Sandy Ridge Academy,' suggested Dee. She named the town and the roads for Doug, too, then stretched out on her stomach, closed her eyes and rested from her labors. She was just a couple of winks from being asleep when Michael's sneaker nudged her bare foot.

'You want anything from the Seven-Eleven?'

Dee rolled on to her side, shading her eyes as she peered up at him. 'Dad put you on break detail, did he?'

'Yes, well, our Kelly girl was sleeping on the job.'

His easy banter eased Dee's humiliation over her father's outburst and her tearful reaction to it. She shook off the last remnant of embarrassment. 'We'd come with you, except if Dad sees us going, he'll call you back in, and you look like you could use a break.'

'Not at all. I'm keeping up pretty good.' He grinned, nearly cocky for Michael.

'Mike? I was hoping you hadn't left yet. Make that a grape soda,' Dee's dad called from the house.

'Okay. I was just going,' Michael was suddenly all business.

'Grape for me, too,' Doug shooed a fly off his leg.

'Dee?'

'Grape's fine.'

Dee moved her beach towel into the sun while

193

Michael was gone. She went inside for her sunglasses and some tanning lotion. When she came back outside, Tulip Johnson was crouched beside Doug at the sand pile. A big silk sunflower adorned the black sailcloth hat on her head. She was wearing a purple tube top under her cut-off painter's coveralls. One strap of the coveralls hung loose, revealing a small tulip tattoo just below her left shoulder blade. Muscles flexed across the wide smooth plane of her shoulders as she pushed Doug's play school bus up Information Highway.

'Is it a hospital?' Dee heard Doug ask.

'No. It's a place where people go to for relief when things get to be too much.' Tulip twisted around, looking up at Dee. 'Hi, Dee. How's it going?'

'Okay, I guess. What're you guys talking about?'

'I was telling Doug about Rosewood and how the people there like it when kids come to visit. We're going to have a bubble bash Saturday morning. I thought maybe he'd like to come,' invited Tulip.

Feeling the way he did about Mr Kolupa, Dee was certain Doug wouldn't set foot inside Rosewood. She sat down on her towel, uncapping the tanning lotion and gave him an easy out. 'Doug's been pretty busy helping Dad work next door. Michael's anxious to get it done so his grandpa can come home again.'

'So I heard,' said Tulip. 'Mike's why I came, actually. But Doug says he's on a soda run.'

'He should be back any second.' Suddenly uneasy, Dee asked, 'Is something wrong with Mr Kolupa?'

'No, no. He's fine,' said Tulip.

Doug peered at her from beneath his hard hat. predictably, he asked, 'Did they fix him?'

'He's not broken, not in the way that you mean.' Angling him an intuitive glance, Tulip asked, 'Does he scare you?'

Doug tucked his head and busied himself tunneling a car through the sand.

'Sometimes when we're scared, it's because we don't understand. Phew-phew.' Tulip spat in the sand, patted it down, then drew the shape of a tulip with a stick. 'Mr K's sloughing. You know, kind of like that scab on your knee. In a day or two, it'll slough. If you don't pick it off first.'

Doug's hand flew to his knee. 'Slough?' he echoed.

'Sure. Take this school bus, for instance. Let's call it K-Bus. See, he goes all over Sand Town picking up kids.' Tulip crawled clear around the sand pile, making puttering sounds as she pushed the bus along. 'Then it climbs School Street. . .'

'That's Information Highway,' corrected Doug.

'. . .to the school.'

'That's the airport,' he interrupted again.

'Oh, really? It should be the school.'

Dee saw Michael pull into the drive and climb out. But Tulip was so busy rearranging Doug's town, she was slow to notice his approach. Having stationed the wooden blocks for the school at the top of the sand pile and another one for the airport at the bottom, she dusted her hands and continued. 'Anyway, K-Bus chugs up the hill. He's made about a zillion runs, but this is his last one because his parts are trashed. He wasn't made to last for ever, you know, and through no fault of his own, he starts sloughing. He sloughs his horn. He can't beep a warning. His mirrors go next. No hindsight now. Then maybe his. . .'

'Steering-wheel?' offered Doug, getting into it.

'Right! Nix the guidance system.' Tulip paused to acknowledge Michael with a grin. 'So where's my soda?'

'Didn't know you were here. Here, take mine,' Michael offered easily.

'Thanks, but no thanks, I'm strictly a diet cola girl. Besides, I'm not staying long.'

'You can't go, you didn't finish your story,' objected Doug as he accepted his grape pop from Michael.

'The story, right!' Tulip scratched her chin and picked up where she left off. 'For sure, K-Bus isn't what it used to be, and sometimes he's pretty bummed out. The kids who rode him have grown up, and K-Bus is pretty much a downer for them. See, he reminds them that some day they'll be antiques, too.'

A light came on in Doug's eyes. 'Oh! K-Bus is an *antique*.'

Tulip beamed. 'Correct-o! He's one of a kind.'

'Then he costs a lot,' said Doug knowingly.

'Priceless,' Tulip agreed. 'But the grown-up kids can't get a clue, they're so busy trying to patch him up and make him be what he used to be. So K-Bus goes to a safe place where they keep him out of the rain and out of the traffic and spiffed up pretty good. Let's call it. . .' Tulip cut a direct gaze Michael's way. 'Buswood.'

Seeing Michael flinch, Dee stirred uncomfortably and tried to change the subject. 'Your hands are filthy, Doug. Run inside and wash before you drink that soda.'

Crouched down, balancing his can of soda between his bend knees, Doug ignored her altogether. He gazed intently at Tulip. 'Is K-Bus happy there?'

'The folks at Buswood give it their all,' said Tulip. 'The driver comes by now and then just to pat the dash. The grown-up students, too. They give him good moments. And once in a blue moon, his headlights flicker and he gives a rusty beep. ''Radical! He's better,'' they think. But then the lights go out, and he's just such a sorry heap, his friends get down all over again.'

Doug jutted out his chin, insisting, 'Why can't the driver fix him? Or the people at Buswood?'

Tulip rested on her haunches and peered at Doug a long moment. 'Smiles.'

'Huh?'

'There! You've got a new tooth coming in.'

Right away, Doug poked his tongue in the space

where the white speck was showing.

'When the old one fell out, did you stick it back in and try and make it stay?' asked Tulip.

Doug grinned. 'That's silly.'

'Well then, see?' exclaimed Tulip.

Looking on, it was doubtful to Dee that Doug *did* see. Michael, on the other hand, clearly got the point. A muscle tightened his jaw, his shoulders stiffened. Dee thought he'd walk away.

'Now and then, K-Bus sees, and while he's sloughed too much to remember, he was all his life storing up unseen treasures for what's yet to come.' Tulip rushed on with her story, aware she was about to lose the main man in her audience. 'But the driver and the grown-up kids see only the hole that will be left when K-Bus is gone.'

'Where is K-Bus going? What happens to him?' asked Doug, unaware of the undercurrents.

Tulip scratched leaves and a stem on to her tulip in the sand and didn't answer.

Doug scrunched up his mouth, thinking. 'Does he go away? Does he die?'

'A lot of people call it that. Others don't want to talk about it or think about what it means.'

'He's seven, Tulip,' Dee intervened, though more on Michael's account than Doug's.

Hands open, palms up, Tulip shrugged. 'I rest my case.'

'Doug's too young, that's all I'm saying,' she defended her attempt to shut Tulip up.

'We're never too young. It's like with tulips.'

Tulip tugged at the brim of her sunflower hat and pointed to her drawing in the sand. 'They're drop-dead-gorgeous when they bloom. Then the petals fade and fall away and the leaves turn brown. If you didn't know those dried-up leaves were feeding something unseen, you'd think it was all over.'

'I get the picture,' Dee said, as abruptly, Michael turned for the house. Lowering her voice, she added, 'But it's got nothing to do with me.'

'It's got to do with all of us. We may not end up at the same stop, but we all take the ride.' Tulip dusted the sand from her hands and glanced at her watch. 'I'm off for the Plaza. Just one more thing. Tell Mike to go visit his grandfather.'

'It isn't my place,' said Dee.

'You're taking up space on the planet, aren't you? Then do your part.'

Dee wagged her head and said bluntly, 'No offense, Tulip, but sometimes you're full of it.'

Tulip smiled, not the least offended. But instead of letting up, she insisted, 'Maybe it'd be easier for Mike if you went with him. Or, if he flat refuses, *you* go. And take your roadie here along with you.' She plucked the silk flower off her hat and gave it to Doug.

Thoroughly irked with her without quite knowing why, Dee said stiffly, Mr Kolupa doesn't know us any more.'

'So? Just be who he thinks you are. He likes that best, anyway.' Tulip rose to her feet, knocked on Doug's hard hat and grinned. 'It's been fun playing with you. Hope to see you at Buswood.'

'It isn't going to happen,' Dee called after her.

Clinging to his sunflower, Doug watched Tulip saunter across the yard, over the sidewalk and to her car. 'Who is she?' he asked finally.

'Tulip Johnson, the weirdest girl I know.'

'She's nice though,' Doug took off his hat and looked for a place to affix the sunflower. Finding none, he wiped his sweaty brow with his arm, dropped to his knees and poked it in the sand next to the tulip Tulip had drawn, 'Look, a flower garden. Play with me, Dee. Okay?'

Dee watched Tulip drive away. She let out the breath she'd been holding. She was unsettling, Tulip was. And it wasn't just the weirdness.

Michael gave Dee's dad his grape pop, and swallowed the last of his own. His belly was fizzing, though not from the soda. He flung the empty can toward the trash bucket in the corner. Darn Tulip anyway! Tracking him down, thinking just because she volunteered a few hours a week at Rosewood, she knew the score. He didn't care what she said, Grandpa deserved a lot more than just 'moments'. More than food and shelter and safety within confining walls. And trying to hold on to him as long as he could wasn't *either* like trying to shove a baby tooth back into your mouth. What a dumb analogy!

He glanced up to see Dee in the doorway. She tested her dad's mood with a quick glance, then shot him an identical glance before perching on a nearby saw horse.

'Doug's made a pretty cool village. You ought to take a look, Dad,' she tried to ditch her father.

Michael flushed and dropped his gaze from her probing look. Luckily, Bob didn't catch the hint. Or if he did, he ignored it. The break was a brief one, and once they'd gone back to work, Dee drifted away. Michael didn't see her again until quitting time, and even then, Alice was with her. Thursday the brick masons were underfoot, working on the fireplace. Dee didn't come over at all. On Friday, she and Doug climbed in a car with Sally Simmons and were gone most of the day.

The brick masons finished up inside and cleared out late in the afternoon. They planned to return on Monday to work on the chimney. Anxious to get the place ready for the drywall tapers, Michael and Bob worked almost until dark hanging the sheet-rock on the walls flanking the new fireplace. If they kept on at this rate, they should have the place habitable by next weekend. According to Bob, anyway.

Pleased with the progress, Michael hung around a while, picking up tools, sweeping and telling Dee's dad a little about his plans for a neon room in Grandpa's tailor shop.

'Takes a manifold to make a neon, doesn't it? I'd think that'd be pretty pricey,' said Bob.

'Not if I build it myself,' said Michael. 'I figure I can make it out of copper or glass, maybe. I'd like to get the room built first, and a good-sized workbench for mounting my fires. Then I'll worry about the equipment.'

'Sounds like you know what you're doing,' said Bob.

'I've been giving it a lot of thought,' Michael admitted. 'It'll take a while to earn enough to get started. But I'd sure appreciate it if you'd check the building out for me, and give me some point-ers.'

'Be glad to.' Bob wound an extension cord into a neat coil, and talked awhile longer before bidding him good-night.

Michael turned off the lights and locked up the house. Steps lagging, he was on his way to his truck when he saw Dee in the porch swing next door. Just looking at her worked like a tonic. He waved and crossed the dewy grass, his weariness easing.

'You want to grab a bite to eat somewhere? I can go home and clean up.'

She paid him swift scrutiny by street light, uncurled her long legs from beneath her, and said with a baiting smile, 'I don't mind slumming it. Just let me get some shoes and tell Mom I'm leaving. Come on in. It's muggy out here,' she added, hold-ing the door for him.

The cool air felt good after the long, hot day. Dee gestured toward the sofa on her way through the living-room. 'Sit down, I'll be right back.'

Certain his shoes were dusty, Michael stayed in the tiled foyer. He could hear bath water running down the hall. Doug was nowhere to be seen. Alice, neither, though her voice was coming in loud and clear from the direction of the kitchen.

He could tell by the wheedling note she had no idea there was anyone other than family on the premises.

'I don't see why not. It isn't a car date. Please, Mom,' she pleaded.

'You're only thirteen, Alice,' Dee's mom's voice held studied patience.

'What's age got to do with it? I know how to handle myself.'

'The biggest part of handling yourself is showing good judgement. Look at you! How long were you in the sun yesterday, anyway?' Dee's mom turned the tables on her.

'A couple of hours is all. It doesn't hurt. Honest. Now about Carl. . .'

'Dee didn't date until she was fifteen.'

'Sixteen. But leave me out of it,' Michael heard Dee say.

'Wait a second, Dee. Tell Mom Carl's harmless,' Alice's disembodied voice entreated.

'As in Carl Simmons? Give it up, Alice.'

'Are you going somewhere?' Dee's mom asked.

'Michael and I are taking off for a while.'

'You won't be late?'

'I don't think so. But I'll call if plans change.'

'Oh, right! She comes and goes as she pleases and I can't even go to one little pool party. That's really fair.'

Dee was fighting a grin as she came through the living-room. She grabbed her pocketbook off the piano and followed him out the door. 'Carl

Simmons, did you hear? The sun must have baked Alice's brain, too. You should see her. She's burnt to a crisp. "Sloughing" as Tulip would say.'

Anxious not to let the conversation stall on Tulip, Michael threw his tool belt into the back of the pick-up truck and dusted the seat off for her. 'One of us isn't slumming it. Is that new?' He gave her dotted-print camp shirt and matching shorts an appreciative glance.

She nodded, looking pleased he'd noticed. 'Sally and I dragged Doug to the mall this morning. We shopped till we dropped all out of cash. May the winds blow and flags unravel!'

'That's the spirit.' He grinned, then asked, as he pulled on to the street, 'Where do you want to eat?'

'How about the Plaza?'

'Anywhere but that,' Michael quickly amended.

She slid him a knowing glance. 'Avoiding Tulip, are we?'

His face heated up.

'You don't have to talk about it if you don't want to,' she said quietly. 'I know! Let's get a pizza.'

'Good idea. We'll take it to the shop. Mom can keep you company while I clean up,' he added. 'You want to pick up a video, too?'

Dee readily agreed. She phoned for the pizza from the video store, then phoned her mother, too. By the time they'd picked out a movie neither of them had seen, the pizza was ready. Once home, Michael invited Mom to share a slice with them. She declined the pizza, but kept Dee company while he cleaned up.

The movie wasn't all that great and the conversation wasn't as easy as it might have been, for though they were alone, Michael couldn't forget Mom was right on the other side of the partition, able to hear every word they said. He slid his arm around Dee's shoulder and said in a hush, 'You want to sit outside?'

'Fire escape?' she whispered back, and smiled when he nodded. 'Sure.'

Leaving the movie running, they tiptoed back through the apartment and let themselves out through the kitchen. The breeze was cool and light, carrying with it the scent of Dee's hair as they sat together on the top step. The conversation was general at first, and quietly spoken. Dee told him of a letter she'd received from Georgia, who was at camp. He, in turn, told her of her Dad offering to help with the neon shop.

'I'm not surprised. He's got a short fuse sometimes, but his bark is worse than his bite.'

Remembering the sawdust incident, Michael slipped his hand in hers. 'He's real proud of you. Alice and Doug, too. I can tell.'

Her hair brushed his cheek as she nodded. 'It'd be nice, though, if he'd say it once in a while.'

'That's hard for him, huh?'

'You better believe it. Mom reads him like a book. Seems to work for her. But sometimes I think for the rest of us, she should make him try to say what he's feeling instead of keeping everything bottled up inside until he explodes.' She angled him a loaded glance. 'Don't you think?'

Heat swept up his neck, for the look in her eyes seemed to be saying more than her words. 'I guess.' Hoping to avoid further discussion, he slipped an arm around her.

She nestled against him and turned her face up. 'You mean that? Because you do it too?'

'Do what?'

'Keep things bottled.'

'When?' he challenged.

'Mostly, when I mention your grandpa.'

He sighed. 'Dee, don't start.'

'See?' she said, retreating a little.

He battled natural defenses, for her closeness stirred in him the desire to please. But how could he tell her of feelings he had yet to sort out himself? That he couldn't do enough to repay Grandpa for all he'd done for him. That he was anxious for him to come home, and yet worried over whether he could be patient enough and watchful enough and loving enough. That he felt guilty for being freed of the responsibility this week. A guilt that got even worse when Tulip said Grandpa kept asking for him. Worse, because he couldn't make himself go to that place. He couldn't. He just couldn't. And there was that quieter voice contradicting his nobler side. . .

'It's difficult, you know?' he said finally.

'I'll go with you to see him, if you'd like,' she offered.

'When would I go? We've worked late almost every night.'

'Only because you want to. If you wanted to go see him, you could.'

'Getting the work done so he can move home is more important in the long run,' Michael said in a way he hoped would end the discussion.

She was quiet so long, the knot in his stomach eased. He buried his face in her hair and whispered, 'I love you, Dee. I have for the longest time.'

Her eyes widened, but she couldn't have been more surprised than he. He hadn't a clue where the words came from. They were true, though. As true as any he'd ever spoken.

She started to speak, but quickly he covered her mouth with a gentle hand. 'Before you say anything, remember – it was you who wanted feelings.'

This time, when she turned up her face, he got the kiss he'd been wanting. It went over him like a slow sweet ache, and he whispered the words again.

Chapter 15

'I've been giving Michael lots of space this week, in case he wanted to back off before this thing between us goes any further. For two days, he made no effort to see me. Which had me kind of worried. Actually, a whole lot worried that maybe he'd had a change of heart. I couldn't have been more wrong! Tonight, he said, "I love you, Dee. I have for the longest time." Those were his exact words. Wow! I didn't say I loved him too. It's too soon. I'm not sure yet, and I want to be sure because he didn't say the words lightly and I don't want to either.'

I can't sleep with that light in my eyes,' Alice complained from across the room. 'What're you writing now?'

'Recipes. I'm almost done.' hurriedly, Dee scrawled, 'Alice is in a foul mood because Mom says she's too young to date. The way I see it, she's still ahead of the game. Boys wouldn't even look at me when I was her age. Come to think of it, thirteen was a lousy year. I was taller than anyone in my class. Dad was on my case all the time about standing up *straight. It was a clothes war with Mom, we couldn't agree on anything. Definitely not a good year.'*

'I'm counting to three, then I'm throwing my show at your lamp,' warned Alice.

'Okay, okay.' There was so much in Dee's head, she could have gone on and on. But she bowed to Alice's nagging and hid her journal under a pile of papers in her desk drawer. She was about to crawl between the sheets and hit the lamp switch when Doug stumbled in.

'What's the matter?' asked Dee.

He squinted and rubbed his eyes. 'I had a bad dream.'

'For crying out loud! Go tell Mom,' ordered Alice.

'She's asleep. Dad told me to go back to bed.'

'Then what're you doing in here?'

Dee ignored Alice and stretched out a hand. 'Come here, Doug. Tell me about your dream.'

'Fine for you, you can lay in bed all morning. I have to work,' Alice snapped the sheet up to her chin.

'No you don't. Tomorrow's Saturday. You can sleep in as long as you want,' Dee reminded.

'I'd still like to get some sleep.'

Alice just couldn't stand not to have the last word. Dee ignored her and patted Doug's knee as he perched on the bed beside her. 'So what was your dream about?'

Doug shot Alice a wary glance, urged Dee closer with a curl of his finger, and whispered, 'Mr

Kolupa was in the basement. He had my watch.'

'How come?' asked Dee.

Doug shrugged. 'I don't know. I woke up.'

'Sometimes, if you make up an ending for a dream, it isn't scary any more.'

'It isn't?'

'Huh-uh. You want to try it?'

'Dee!' whined Alice. 'Take it somewhere else!'

Dee sighed. 'Come on, we'll go in your room so the troll can hibernate.'

'Will you sleep with me?'

'For a while.'

'Better take your hip waders.' Alice flounced over in bed, her back to them both.

'Go on,' Dee motioned to Doug. 'I'll be right there.' As soon as he'd gone, she crossed the room, jerked Alice's pillow from beneath her head and whacked her with it.

Alice bolted up in bed, yelping, 'What's that for?'

'Because you're so mean!'

'All I said was. . .'

'I heard. And it was mean.'

'He's going to be a big sissy if you don't quit babying him,' Alice defended.

'So I should be mean too, then he can hate both of us?'

Hurt flashed in Alice's eyes. But it quickly hardened into anger. 'Like you're so perfect. You could have stuck up for me with Mom, you know. She might have made an exception.'

Baffled, Dee asked, 'What are you babbling about?'

'Going to the swim party with Carl.'

'Carl Simmons is Michael's age.'

'So what?'

'He's too old for you, that's what.'

'See what I mean? You make me sick!'

'Alice, knock it off and go to sleep,' Dad called from his bedroom down the hall.

'Now see what you've done!' Alice's voice dropped from a shriek to an injured whisper.

'Me?' cried Dee indignantly.

'It's always me that gets yelled at.' Tears sprang to Alice's eyes. She pulled the sheet over her head. 'I hate you, Dee. I hate you, I hate you, I hate you.'

Her sister's hoarse whisper stunned like a quick, sharp blow. Dee dropped the pillow and turned away. Not so long ago, when Dad had hollered after lights out, it was because they were jumping on their beds, talking, giggling. Exchanging secrets instead of insults and angry words. Dee turned in the door, wanting to say something, anything, just so the last word to echo wasn't *hate* and the sleepy contentment of only moments ago would return. But Alice was lying there all stiff and unforgiving. *Forget it. Just let it blow over.*

Dee closed the door quietly. There was a crease of light beneath the bathroom door. Alice's barb had nudged Doug into making a pit stop. She tiptoed on to his room, and sat thinking of Mr Kolupa as she waited. How he lived in the past, often mistaking Michael for his brother Richard, long dead. And in so doing, adopting a fretful, slightly impatient tone. As if it'd been his job to keep his brother in line. What kind of memories had he made? *What kind were she and Alice making?*

Doug padded in to join her. Dee tucked him in, then stretched out on top of the bedspread beside him. He said no more about the dream, so she let it go too, and in a short while, his breathing was light and even.

It wasn't so easy for Dee. She was wide awake now, her pleasure in Michael's words of love diminished by the flare-up with Alice. Glancing at the bathroom clock on her way by, she saw midnight had come and gone. That made it the twenty-fourth. The day of Pru's next diary entry.

Dee collected the diary from her room, then went out to the kitchen. She tucked a marshmallow and some chocolate bits between graham crackers, popped it in the microwave a few seconds and enjoyed a solitary snack before opening Pru's diary.

'*After three days of consistent rain, it is now hot and steamy. The flies are voracious and little Emily fussed all day. Molly and Mildred are worn out from dragging through the mud and the twins got into some kind of poison weed picking flowers and will not stop scratching. The grease in my skillet caught fire and burned supper, and when Molly criticized my cooking, I slapped her. I was so ashamed, I ran off and cried. It was the first time alone I've had since Mother died. Later, Father took me aside, and told me that if the load was too much, he would make an arrangement with a widow woman traveling with the train. The arrangement she spoke of was marriage. I was so startled, I assured him I would work harder at running things smoothly. But I am tired and discouraged and the work is so endless. Part of me would be glad to turn over the responsibility if it didn't mean that someone was taking Mother's place.'*

How fitting, after that scene with Alice! Dee closed the old book, feeling close to Pru. Despite all the changes over the past century and a half, family ties had remained remarkably the same. Sisters still quarreled and repented of quarreling only to quarrel again. And still they were sisters, seamlessly cemented. Or could too much strife erode what they took for granted? Dee rubbed tired eyes, regretting her part in the tiff. She had, after all, implied Doug hate Alice, which wasn't true, for Doug was too sweet-natured to hate anyone. And she'd hit her with the pillow, too. Maybe in the morning she could think of a way to smooth things over.

Stretched out on Grandpa's lumpy sofa, Michael's thoughts were slow to give over to sleep. A week ago, the turmoil over Grandpa had fostered a bleakness within. A weight sucking him down and down until he felt isolated, banished almost, to a narrow tunnel-like place where little light shone.

But tonight, sitting out on the fire escape with Dee, a joy for living stirred, strong and sweet and seductive.

The neon sign lighting the window caught Michael's eye as he turned, trying to get comfortable. Not even the burned-out 'c' bothered him tonight. His plans for a neon shop no longer overwhelmed him now that Bob had agreed to help. The flag business showed promise, too. And the house was coming along a treat. He wasn't going to think any more about Tulip's words. By this time next week, the house should be ready for Grandpa's homecoming and to visit or not to visit would no longer be an issue. His thoughts drifted until sleep carried him swiftly to the morning.

Michael got up to find Mom had left a note: 'Gone to Rosewood. Why don't you stop by today and say hello to Grandpa? Love, Mom.'

Michael crumpled the note in his hand, bounded down the stairs and stopped for donuts on his way to the house. He pottered around a bit, but without Bob there, his limited knowledge on what needed doing next soon caught up with him. Maybe he'd go next door. If Dee was up, they could cruise the town, see if there were any flags needing mending. A little early yet, though.

Rosewood. The thought picked at him like a mouse nibbling at cheese. He resisted it and poked about his bedroom for a while. With both his computer and the TV at Grandpa's place, there wasn't much diversion to be found.

Rosewood. No! He addressed the thought directly. *Why not? You've got time on your hands*, his conscience nagged.

It's a downer, a bummer, a warehouse, a gaol. It's 'what is', for Grandpa, if for some reason his plans to bring him home fell through. *Why would they fall through?* Because, deep down, the quiet voice was growing more insidious. More persistent. More articulate.

Uneasy with his thoughts, Michael strode next door. Dee was up and dressed and agreeable to the flag plan. They picked up half a dozen, sewed them all and took them back again, then ate a late lunch before returning to Dee's house. Dee's mother was outside working in her flower bed. Doug was at a friend's house and Alice was on her way out, planning to meet Yolanda at the mall.

Michael settled beside Dee on the living-room sofa. They were watching TV when all at once Dee snapped her fingers and jumped up. 'I just remembered! Pru's diary. Today's the day.'

'Her next entry? Bet you read it without me, didn't you?' Michael got up off the sofa and followed her down the hall, then paused on the threshold of her room. He was surprised to find Alice's side nearly as neat as Dee's. 'What happened in here?'

'I picked up a little.'

'What's the matter – the loan shark calling in her debts again?'

Dee chuckled as she withdrew the diary from

216

her desk. Leading the way back to the living-room, she confided, 'Actually, it was Pru's entry that inspired me to do Alice's half of the room. Plus, I got to thinking about being thirteen and how it wasn't all that great. See, we had this big fight...Oh, never mind. Just read. Then you'll understand.'

Michael leafed to the day's entry and read the careful hand of Dee's long-dead ancestor. He understood, all right. Not about Dee cleaning for Alice – *that* was a puzzle. But he sure connected with the helplessness, the flash of temper, the overwhelmed feeling of the writer. Curious to know if Pru had resolved her guilt conflict brought on by too much responsibility, Michael turned the page.

'Huh-uh, no fair looking ahead.' Dee took the book from him, adding, 'Just for the record I didn't slap Alice. I hit her with a pillow. But I felt bad about it afterwards, just like Pru. Alice makes it tough, you know? Being at peace with her, I mean. That rose bowl on my dresser? The one that was growing mould the other day?' she rattled on. 'She poked a sweet potato in it. The water's so black, I wouldn't have noticed, except there's this tiny yellow sprout coming on.'

'Sweet potato? What for?' asked Michael, trying to keep up with her hop, skip and a jump from Pru's diary to Alice to sweet potatoes.

'Mischief.' Dee wagged her head, but her mouth wiggled.

Suspecting she found Alice more amusing than she was willing to concede, Michael said, 'So, what's the joke?'

'It isn't a joke, exactly. See, your mom gave Doug this old corsage. I told him it wouldn't grow, but Doug likes to test things out for himself. So he put it in that rose bowl with some water. Enter Alice and her sweet potato prank. When it leafs out, he'll think the corsage is growing.' She dimpled and added, 'Pru's good influence aside, I may have to clobber the little troll again.'

Amazing! They'd read the same passage, and related to it in totally different ways. But then, he'd never had to figure out how to get along with a sibling. Probably made all the difference.

'What?' prodded Dee, appearing goaded by his smile.

'Nothing. I was just thinking. . .skip it.'

'No, go ahead. What were you thinking?' she pursued it.

'Just that you might want to step back and let Doug and Alice work things out for themselves for a change.'

'I do, mostly,' she claimed. At his shrewd glance, she blushed and amended, 'Well, maybe I don't. But Doug's a lot younger, you know?'

He shrugged. 'Never mind. It's not my call, anyway. So how about catching a movie later?'

She beamed. 'Sure. Sounds great.'

Dee walked him out to his truck. He liked the way that she did that. As if she hated to see him go.

The sweetness of it warmed Michael all the way home. He tidied up the shop downstairs, then climbed the steps to the apartment, intending to clean up for his date with Dee.

The fans were better at drawing in the fumes from the street than at cooling the upstairs. Spotting Mom at the kitchen sink, perspiration gluing her shirt to her back, Michael gave her a wave and grabbed a soda from the refrigerator. 'Miss that central air, don't you?'

'Soft, I tell you!' She smiled, damp ringlets framing her face. 'I haven't seen much of you today. What've you been up to?'

Michael straddled a kitchen chair and cooled his throat while he filled her in on how he'd spent his day.

'Did you get a chance to stop by Rosewood?'

Michael set the can down carefully. 'I told you, Mom. I don't want to go there.'

'This isn't about "wanna", it's about "oughta".' She lifted her shoulder, wiping beaded sweat from her brow. 'He misses you, Michael. He asked about you again today.'

'I miss him too. I'm doing everything I can to see that the house gets finished fast so he can come home.'

'I'm not sure we should bring him home.'

The last sip of pop seemed tepid, sickly sweet in his mouth. 'What do you mean?'

'I mean, leave him at Rosewood. He's adjusting pretty well all things considered.'

There was heat behind his eyes as conflicting emotions duked it out. The magnanimous voice, and the softer wheedling one. Rejecting the second as weak, he stood by his original plan. 'You promised, Mom.'

'I said for the summer,' she kept her voice level. 'By the time the house is ready, the summer will be half gone. I question the wisdom of disrupting him yet again. And for what? A month and a half at the most? Then we're right back where we started.'

'It doesn't have to change at the end of the summer. I'll stay with him as long as he needs me,' Michael protested.

'What about the classes in neon? Remodeling the shop? The flag business?' she asked.

'I don't have to go to school, I can teach myself. Bob's going to help me remodel the shop. Dee and I are working on the flags.' He had an answer for every objection. Except the unspoken ones in his own head. 'I've got a handle on things.'

'Michael, don't you see? You can't even find the time to pay him a visit. There are not enough hours in the day! And yet you're wanting to make this huge sacrifice.'

'It isn't a sacrifice.'

'It is too!' she said, voice escalating unexpectedly. 'It's too much. He's had his life and if he were himself, he would be the last one to want to get in the way of you having yours!'

She was yelling at him, yelling as she held back tears. The anger, he knew, was not so much with him, as with circumstances that forced her to choose between his welfare and Grandpa's. Deep down, the wheedling voice he mistrusted as self-serving echoed her words.

At length, she said in a calmer voice, 'He is my father, Michael. Mine and Sheri's, not yours. Whatever you owe him, we owe him more.' Mom clattered the last dish into the drain, dried her hands and patted his shoulder. 'But Dad would be the last one to make life for us a debt we can't repay. He'd cancel it freely, you know that he would.'

Mom's fingers, draped over his shoulders, blurred. Bitterly, he asked, 'Then why does it feel like abandonment?'

She joined him at the table, sighing as she dropped into the chair. 'Because you're made of the right stuff. I've called you my hero enough times, you're convinced that's the role you have to play. But I never meant it to be a burden. I only mean to say I'm proud of you. And that's not going to change, whatever your choice.'

'*My* choice?' he echoed, head turning.

She nodded. 'If you want it to be. As long as you understand that Dad's condition isn't going to improve. I've read and I've heard from others what is to follow. You should be educating yourself about what to expect.'

Pained, he objected, 'Mom, don't start with that support group scare stuff.'

'I've seen it with my own eyes at Rosewood,' she persisted. 'Paranoia. Catastrophic reactions. Tube

221

feeding. Incontinence.'

He cringed at the pictures her words conjured. 'Then why would you want to leave him there?'

'Because they have the training to handle it in a patient, caring manner. And when necessary, the detachment to cope with what we can't.'

'But it's my choice?'

She nodded. 'There are conditions. I want you to take your time thinking it over. Two, if you decide to bring him home, I reserve the right to say when enough is enough. And three, I want you to go see him at Rosewood. No, listen,' she added, when he started to interrupt. 'You can't make an educated decision without a clear understanding of both options.'

It was settling on him again. Sucking him down like gravity. *He couldn't go there. He couldn't.*

'Michael?' she pressed gently.

He dropped his head into his hands, the pressure mounting. Darkness behind his eyelids, pinpricks. He thought he'd wanted this. Now suddenly, he resented the weight of it all. The ponderous magnitude of deciding for another person. *She was wrong. He wasn't made of the right stuff. Not by a long shot.*

'I'll go with you, if you like,' she offered.

He blurted, 'Doesn't seeing those old ones sick and broken-down and with nothing to do and nowhere to go. . ..doesn't it. . .'

'Break your heart?' she finished for him.

Not his exact thoughts, but close enough.

She laced fingers still red and puckered from the dish water. 'In a way, yes. But who's to say broken hearts aren't like broken bones? Maybe after the healing, they're sounder than ever.'

'Sounds like one of Tulip's analogies.' Provoked by the reminder of Tulip's butting in, he repeated her example of the baby tooth.

Mom's mouth relaxed into a quiet smile. 'I think I like that girl.'

'You would. She's nuts, too,' said Michael. But he said it without rancor, for though he couldn't admit it out loud, one of Tulip's analogies had proved comfortingly familiar – the one about dying foliage storing up unseen treasures for the spring.

Grandpa had taught him as much about people storing up treasures in an unseen beyond. People who, by conscious choice, look to the needs of others and plod faithfully through every trial life hurls. Though he hadn't said so aloud, that was a large part of the conflict within. The two voices. One urging him to look after himself, the other to look after Grandpa. Mom could gloss over it and say Grandpa wouldn't expect it. But the seed was planted by Grandpa's own hand. He should plod on.

Am I right, God? Is that what I should do?

The silence was deafening.

Chapter 16

'Michael's house is done. He's going to move their stuff back from the upstairs apartment this morning. The expanded living-room with the fireplace is gorgeous. Alice and I helped Paula paint over the weekend. Mom was going to help, too, but she just got her cast off and her foot's pretty weak.

Alice tagged along with Michael and me to the Plaza last night for burgers and sodas. It was Sally's day off. Tulip waited on us, wouldn't you know? When she brought our ticket, she started in on Michael about going to see his grandpa. It was getting tense when Alice spots Carl across the restaurant teasing a red-haired waitress in painted on jeans. The troll – oops, I mean Alice (I'm making a real effort) -sticks her nose in the air and claims she doesn't care, that Carl was just a phase, anyway. This boy from her class at school was sitting at the next table. He must have been listening, because right away he comes over and asks Alice if she'd like to play some pinball down in the game room. That stroked her ego. Michael and I joined them. It was fun, even if Alice did out-score me big-time.'

Dee stopped to wipe an ink blotch off the page. Between babysitting with Doug and helping paint next door she'd fallen behind in her journal. Michael was going to stop by soon to give her and Doug a ride downtown. Bent on catching up in the meantime, she traded the pen for one that didn't leak and resumed writing.

'Tomorrow, for Independence Day, Paula's having a cookout. She says it's in appreciation of Dad's speedy job, and the whole family is invited. Her sister Sheri and her family are coming too. And Mr Kolupa. Michael's mum on the subject, but I guess he's planning on his grandpa coming back to live with them again now that the house is done. According to Mom, Paula wants him to visit Rosewood first and understand the care Mr Kolupa is getting. I don't know why Michael hasn't been to see his grandfather. I've tried to ask him, but he won't talk about it. Maybe it shouldn't bother me, but it does because I think we should be able to share what's bugging us.'

'Dee? Michael's here,' Doug called from the front of the house.

Dee tucked her journal away, raked a comb through her hair and hurried out to meet him. Michael looked happy to see her. He squeezed her hand as they walked to the truck and said he was glad he'd called and asked for a lift. But he seemed preoccupied. A short while later, he would have driven right past the jewelers if Dee hadn't spoken up.

'Sorry. Wasn't thinking.' Michael pulled over to the curb. Doug leaped out and raced into the jeweler's without waiting for her.

Dee slid across the seat to the door, then paused to ask, 'Do you want some help moving your stuff back to the house?'

'I brought most of it on my way over. Anyway, I've got to hang around the shop a while. Your dad's going to stop by and offer me some advice on the neon room.'

'I thought he was pouring footings today,' said Dee.

'Later this morning. I'm going to help.'

'Watch out, he'll get used to it.'

Michael returned her smile. 'He's willing to help me out, so I figure I better do what I can for him now.'

'Sounds like a plan.' Dee climbed out, then turned back to wave. 'Thanks for the lift. See you.'

Doug had already presented the jeweler with the claim ticket. He had the watch in hand by the time Dee made it to the counter. She paid the repair fee and followed him out into the sunshine.

Head down, fingering the watch, he stopped in front of Livingston's Variety Store and held it up to her ear. 'Listen!'

His enchantment with the thing made her smile. 'Pretty cool. The chain's the crowning touch, huh. Here, let me help.'

Dee was attaching the chain to the loop on Doug's cut-off shorts when Tulip burst out of

Livingston's and held the door for Mr Oppenheimer. Spotting Dee, she asked without prelude, 'Have you got a car?'

'No. Why?' asked Dee cautiously.

'We took the bus. Mr Oppie's suddenly feeling bad and it's an hour before we can catch the bus back.'

Dee took a closer look at Tulip's aged companion. He was breathing hard and he looked kind of unsteady. 'Does he need an ambulance?'

'I think what he needs most is to rest. He's got a respiratory thing. The sultry air makes it worse.' Tulip led Mr Oppenheimer to a nearby bench and fanned him with her black sailcloth hat.

'I'll get Mom's car. It's just two blocks.'

'Thanks, Dee.' Tulip raised her voice, assuring the elderly gentleman. 'We're getting a ride in just a few minutes. Here, Doug. Keep fanning him while I loosen his collar. Just relax. Catch your breath. That's the way, Mr Oppie.'

Dee made it back with the car in record time. She was relieved to see Mr Oppenheimer's color had improved. She cranked up the air. By the time they reached Rosewood, the old fellow was admiring Doug's 'new' old watch.

'You're coming in, aren't you?' asked Tulip, as she helped Mr Oppenheimer from the car.

'Wasn't planning on it,' Dee admitted.

'But you're already here. You may as well drop in and say hello to Mr Kolupa.'

At Tulip's insistence, Dee parked the car in the

visitors' lot and went in. The lobby was bright and cheerfully decorated with the artwork of the residents. Men and women, some in wheelchairs and walkers, stared at them with varying degrees of interest. Tulip turned Mr Oppenheimer over to a nurse, then beckoned, saying, 'Mr Kolupa's room is this way. Come on, I'll show you.'

The corridor was long, and Tulip didn't pass a single resident without a pat or a greeting or a word of encouragement. Looking on, Dee was reminded of a professional entertainer warming up the crowd. The more gregarious ones smiled and fussed over Doug. One sturdy fellow with watery eyes and an energetic gait gripped Doug's hand and introduced himself.

'Oscar Payton from Riverton.'

The man shook Dee's hand and repeated, 'Oscar Payton from Riverton.'

'Oscar Payton from Riverton,' he said once again, reaching for Tulip's hand.

'Nice to meet you, Mr Payton,' said Tulip, as if it were their first time.

As they walked on, Dee heard Mr Payton introduce himself to a maintenance man who was buffing the floor. Beside her, Doug jumped as a shrill voice rang from the nearest room.

'Get out! Get out!'

Dee glanced in the open door. A frail little white-haired lady was picking through a small box containing what looked like keepsakes. She was holding it just out of reach of a woman in a wheelchair.

'Put it back! Get out of my things!' bleated the second woman.

Tulip darted into the sunny room. The one in the wheelchair lifted her face, entreating, 'Tell her, Mother. Tell her to leave my things alone!'

'Why, it's Betsy. Sweet Betsy from Pike.' With a smile and a song, Tulip diverted the tiny bright-eyed woman from her pilfering and coaxed her into the corridor. Betsy allowed herself to be led along a few paces before flitting as light as air down the hall ahead of them.

'Should we catch her?' whispered Doug, brow furrowed.

'It wouldn't do any good,' said Tulip. 'Betsy's like a butterfly. She lights where she lights.'

She led them past a glass wall. In the dining-room on the other side, a young man in white was spoon-feeding an elderly woman in a wheelchair. 'Open your mouth, Ruby. Just one more bite,' Dee heard him coax. The woman sat as still and silent as a shuttered window. Dee hurried past, nearly overrunning Tulip as she stopped to knock on a closed door.

'Mr Kolupa? Would you like some company?' Tulip swept the door wide and ushered them in. This room, too, was full of sunshine. A radio on the bedside table was turned down so low it was barely audible. Mr Kolupa was in a chair, fully dressed. He searched Tulip's face, then Dee's, with no sign of recognition. But when he spotted Doug, even the wrinkles on his bald head creased with his smile.

'Michael! Let's have a look at you!' He stretched out a hand, inviting Doug to draw closer.

Doug hung back, pressing against Dee. Trying for Doug's sake to hide her own awkward feelings, Dee edged closer. 'Hello, Mr Kolupa. I'm Michael's friend, Dee. This is my brother, Doug.'

Still beaming, Mr Kolupa patted his knee. 'Come sit on my lap. Wait till she sees you. She's going to. . .she'll think. . .she'll be glad.'

'You guys have a nice visit. I'm going to check on Mr Oppie,' Tulip sailed back out the door.

Oh, great! Now they were stuck. Wondering how to fill the silence, Dee perched on the only other chair in the room and pulled Doug down beside her. 'How are you feeling, Mr Kolupa?'

'He says I'm doing fine. He comes here sometimes to. . .it isn't so. . .you know.' He frowned and moved his hand as if erasing a slate. 'Find him something to. . .he should have a. . .he needs play.'

Realizing he meant Doug, Dee said, 'He's fine. Aren't you, Doug?'

Doug nodded. But Mr Kolupa got out of his chair and opened a bureau drawer. 'Where is it? It was right here. It was here.' He jerked out the drawer and dumped undershirts and boxer shorts all over the bed.

Seeing his frustration mount, Dee grabbed a photo album off the table and tried to divert his attention as Tulip had done with Betsy. The photos were black and white, the fashions of an earlier era. 'What neat pictures. Tell me about this one.'

She pointed to a young man on a bicycle.

Mr Kolupa took the book from her and sat down. 'That's him. He's over there.'

'What a pretty house. Who is the girl?'

Dee turned the pages one at a time, asking questions about each picture. Mr Kolupa's replies were pretty much meaningless, for he used pronouns instead of names and places.

Bored, Doug wandered to the bedside table and fidgeted with the radio. As the volume shot up, Mr Kolupa raised his head. Pictures forgotten, he got to his feet and started to dance. It was the same slow shuffle he'd done at graduation. Doug crept a little closer, his offishness fading. When the music faded into a commercial and Mr Kolupa stopped shuffling, he said, 'You're a good dancer.'

Mr Kolupa gestured toward a framed picture on his bedside table. It was of his wife in her youth. 'She taught me. She loved to dance.'

'Mrs Kolupa?' asked Dee, for his eyes seemed clearer and his thought more connected.

'I should have gone. But there was work. And the children.'

He dropped his head, looking regretful and lonesome and suddenly tired. They had stayed long enough. Perhaps he, like Mr Oppie, needed to rest. Dee got to her feet.

'It'll be time for lunch soon. We should be going.'

'Where's my. . .it should be. . .' Mr Kolupa sifted through the clothes he'd spilled on to the bed.

Taking a pair of boxer shorts, he sat down and worked at fitting a shoe through one leg hole.

Feeling awkward, Dee returned the rest of the clothes to the drawer. 'You don't need those, Mr Kolupa. Here, let me help you put them away,' she said hesitantly.

Bent once, clinging stubbornly to the shorts, he panted, 'I can do it.'

'Dee?'

Dee swung around to see Michael filling the doorway. Her own surprise was mirrored in his face.

'What're you doing here?'

'We gave Tulip a lift. What about you? I thought you were working with Dad.'

'He doesn't need me until after lunch.' Michael looked past her to his grandfather. No longer hampered by Dee's interference, Mr Kolupa was pulling the boxer shorts up over his trousers. A dark stain flooded Michael's face. His mouth tightened.

'You had to come, didn't you. You couldn't leave it alone.'

Dee's heart shrank at the accusing note in his voice. *What had she done to make him so angry?* Bewildered, she defended. 'I didn't plan it. Though what difference that would make. . .' She faltered, heat sweeping her face, 'Michael, you're not being. . .'

'What? Being what?'

His eyes were like vapors boiling off dry ice. Feelings bruised, hot tears pressed for release.

Dee darted past him into the corridor. He made no attempt to stop her. Seconds later, Doug's racing steps caught up with her. He sneaked a sidelong glance, then slipped his hand into hers.

'Hey! What's the matter? Where's the fire?' Tulip called as they streaked through the lobby.

Dee rushed out the door and didn't look back.

Why had he come? He shouldn't have come. It was worse, much worse than he'd imagined. Wheelchairs and walkers. A woman down the hall, weeping for mother. A man clinging to his name and his town. Worn bodies, vacant minds. Pain and passive patience. Waiting, just waiting to die. Michael knotted his fists, despising the cruel truth that Grandpa was just as vacant, just as passive, just as worn as the faces that turned as he passed, seeking some diversion, and diversion from the awful waiting. *What a place to fit in!*

Cold inside, he motioned to Grandpa. 'Take those off. We're getting out of here.'

Child-like, Grandpa turned unquestioningly toward the door.

'You can't go out looking like that. Take them off,' Michael said a second time.

Grandpa kept moving at the same even gait.

Michael grabbed him by the arm. 'Grandpa! Did you hear me? Take off those shorts. You look ridiculous.'

Grandpa swung free and shook his finger at him. 'Watch yourself, Richard.'

'I'm not Richard, I'm Michael. Look at me! Look at me, Grandpa.' He gripped both shoulders and gave him a shake. 'Richard is dead. He's been dead fifty years. I'm Michael. Do you hear?'

'Whoa, there. Time out!' Tulip Johnson sailed in and wedged her strong, square shoulder between him and Grandpa. 'Get a grip, would you?' At his resistance, she added, 'Or did you want to take a swing first?'

Her words went over Michael like cold water. All the fury drained away in a heartbeat. He slumped against the wall, shocked, ashamed, trembling.

'There, there. It was a little misunderstanding that's all. You're fine, aren't you, Mr Kolupa?' Tulip put her bronzed cheek next to Grandpa's and whispered loudly, 'Personally, I think you're stylin'. But, it's laundry day and I need those shorts. Peel them off. That's time. We'll just put them over here until they come for the wash.'

Michael sank into the chair and dropped his head in his hands. *What was he thinking, manhandling Grandpa.* Out of control. A bare wire, zapping everything he touched. Grandpa couldn't help his behavior. But he was without excuse.

Long, blunt-tipped fingers lighted on his shoulder. 'You snapped, okay? It happens.'

Michael sat motionless. Thoughts shying from the ugliness of what he had done, he seized Tulip as a distraction. *What was with her? Why would anyone be here by choice?* He dragged his fingers

235

through his hair. 'How can you stand the dying?' He flushed, for it wasn't what he'd meant to ask.

'You look at it hard and fast and if you're into praying, ask for understanding,' she said evenly.

'I've tried,' he mumbled. 'Sometimes I think I'm just talking to myself. You know?'

'I've been there. It feels like flying blind in a storm. Particularly if you're a control freak.' Tulip commiserated with a sympathetic wag of her head, then chirped, 'But the bottom line is this – it's in God's hands. Turn over the 'stick' and just hang on.'

He angled her a wary glance. 'This isn't going to be an aviation twist on the K-Bus story, is it?'

She grinned, her burnished cheeks balling up like apples. 'Enough said. You're a smart guy.'

A little woman humming an aimless tune paused in Grandpa's open door and held up a teddy bear.

'Betsy, have you been shopping again? Cool teddy bear you've got there. Let me see.' Tulip slipped the bear behind her back and plucked a bright plastic flower out of her pocket. 'Here, Betsy. Put it in your hair. No contest, you're a knock-out!'

Bear forgotten, Betsy admired herself in the mirror a moment, then drifted away, still humming in the high, thin voice. There was a quality to it that made Michael flinch. He lifted his gaze to Tulip and asked bluntly, 'How can you stand it here?'

'They like me,' she said simply. 'Go figure.'

'That's no reason.'

Her gaze slid away. Flippancy retreating, she said, 'My dad was here in the Alzheimer's wing. Six months after he died, Mom remarried. Trevor was part of the package. He's a tough act to follow.'

'Tougher than this?' Michael glanced away as Grandpa shuffled out into the corridor. 'You've got to be kidding.'

'It's nice to be needed. An escape from normality. But enough about me.' Tulip crossed the room, turned the volume up on the radio, and came back again. 'You don't talk about the patient in front of the patient, that's the first rule. There's a lot more to follow. You've gotta learn all you can if you're serious about taking your grandpa home.'

'You're saying I shouldn't?'

'That's not my call. I can tell you though, if you're looking for a guilt-free choice, forget it. You leave him here, you feel you've let him down. You take him home, you don't get enough rest or enough freedom or enough life of your own, the pressure gets to you, and you crack over some little thing like undershorts. I don't have to tell you how that makes you feel.'

He ducked his head, the shame rushing over him again.

Tulip clapped him on the shoulder. 'I've been there a time or two myself. Now, if you're done beating yourself up, take your Grandpa down to the lobby and let him mess with the chairs. He gets off on that, had you noticed?'

'There's a reason,' said Michael.

'There's always a reason. Finding it is the challenge.'

'Yeah, I guess.' He got to his feet, but half-way to the door turned back, struck by how different Tulip seemed at school. Gaudy and audacious and boisterous. Or maybe it was just that he'd never scratched beneath the surface. In the back of his mind, already, he was anxious over Dee. He'd snapped at her, too. But Tulip had seen the worst in him. The very worst. And she wasn't judging. He gazed at her a long moment and noticed for the first time that she was a handsome girl.

'What?' she asked, though he hadn't spoken.

'Thanks, Tulip. You're okay.'

'Finally! Something we can agree on.' She beamed and waved him on.

Chapter 17

'Independence Day is all about freedom, and here I am, stuck in my room avoiding Michael. Alice promised before she left for the cookout to tell him, if he asked, that I hadn't come back yet from visiting Georgia at camp. Sally and I drove up there yesterday afternoon. Georgia looked great and the kids in her cabin all love her, I can tell. We spent the night and drove back a little while ago. I could've stayed out at Sally's tonight. Probably should have – her dad's restocked his supply of fireworks. But I just didn't feel like celebrating.'

Dee glanced up from her journal as across the street a string of firecrackers cracked and popped. Ought to be real good for Mr Kolupa's nerves. He was on the deck next door. She'd watched from behind the curtain a little earlier as he rearranged chairs. But her family and Sheri's family were filling them all now. *Had he come home to stay? Or was he going back to Rosewood?*

Dee quickly withdrew the question as none of her business. Obviously, that's how Michael looked at it. She picked up her pen to resume writing, but couldn't find words to describe just how she felt. Hurt didn't cover it. Neither did mad. Restless, she wandered to the closet, poked her journal down the leg of last winter's boots and slipped out to the kitchen for something to eat. Mom had taken all the good stuff next door for the cookout. She toasted a cheese sandwich beneath the broiler, garnished it in pickles and was on her way back to her room when she heard the door leading in from the garage open.

'Doug?'

He didn't answer, but a moment later, Dee heard a whistle downstairs. Mom had brought home an old electric train from Granny's Attic. According to Alice, Doug and Dad had spent a good part of the afternoon downstairs setting up the track on saw horses and plywood.

Dee ate her sandwich, then closed the mini-blinds before dropping into the window seat with Pru's diary. There wasn't a Fourth of July entry. In fact, there wasn't another entry until the middle of July. She intended only to take a peek. But the first sentence aroused her curiosity and she kept reading.

Imelda Ellis is forty years old, a spinster and strong as any man. She has driven her own wagon, cared for her own stock, and in so doing, won the respect of everyone in the company. Last week the twins picked her some flowers. She came to our campfire later and asked Father if she might have a hand in occupying the younger ones. As if it were a privilege! "Now I ain't hankerin' to be nobody's wife nor mother, mind you! But I wouldn't mind a spot of company." These were her words. The twins in particular have taken to Miss Ellis. They strive to please her by cooperating in a way they have not done since Mother passed away.'

Dee's eyes were skipping ahead to the next entry when Alice let herself in. She said without prelude, 'Michael's not having much fun, I can tell.'

'Did you tell him I was at Sally's?' At Alice's nod, Dee couldn't keep herself from asking, 'What'd he say?'

'He asked when you were coming home?'

'And?' Dee prompted.

'I said I wasn't sure, but it probably wouldn't be late.'

Dee frowned. 'What'd you tell him that for?'

'I don't know, Dee. I guess I felt sorry for him.'

'Thanks a lot.'

'I don't get it,' admitted Alice. 'What'd he do that's so awful?'

'You really want to know?' Dee closed the diary and confided in Alice what she had withheld from Sally and Georgia. 'He won't say what's bugging him, he just keeps it inside. Then poof! He snaps. Just like Dad. I don't even know what it's about. Well, I kind of know,' she admitted. 'But it's no reason for him to blow up at me.'

Doubtful, Alice said, 'I don't think I've ever seen Michael mad.'

241

'Be glad. He isn't loud with it. But he's got a look that'll cut you right down.' Dee crossed to the window facing Michael's house and looked out on his back yard. 'Where is he, anyway?'

Alice joined her for a quick glance. She shrugged. 'Maybe he took Mr Kolupa inside.'

'Is he staying with Paula and Michael again?'

'Search me.' Alice crossed the room and trailed her finger along the dresser as she looked back at Dee. 'You should sneak over while Michael's gone and see Sheri's baby. Little Ira Earl. What a name! He's bald and wrinkly and his hands flit about just like Mr Kolupa's. I bet if he could talk, he'd say, "O wretched babe that I am".'

'You're awful,' said Dee, smothering a grin.

Encouraged, Alice expanded her critique. 'If you ask me, Sheri's whole family is bizarre. Her husband gave a blow-by-blow of the baby's delivery. Nasty!' she wrinkled her pert nose. 'And the little girls can't leave their hands off anything. They squirted charcoal lighter on Mom's flowers and smeared ketchup all over Doug's bike. He's hiding from them right now.'

'Huh-uh,' Doug spoke up from the doorway. 'I'm playing with my train. You want to come see, Dee?'

Eyes twinkling, Alice taunted, 'You want me to send the girls down?'

'Don't do it,' Doug said quickly.

'I'll tell them you're giving train rides in the dungeon. All aboard for the abyss.' In the midst of her teasing, Alice stopped short and stared into the murky water blackening the rose bowl. 'Hey, get a load of this. There's something growing in here.'

Dee had been keeping track of the slender shoot. It was about an inch long, now. Doug hadn't noticed it, and she hadn't said a word about it to either one of them. But she'd wondered how long Alice could stand the waiting. Doug, poor gullible kid, was all eyes. Hoping to spare him being the butt of another Alice prank, Dee ambled toward the door. 'Guess I'll go see that train. You coming, Doug?'

'Really! There is,' insisted Alice. 'There's something growing!'

'I'll show you how to run it, then we'll take turns being the engineer, okay?' asked Doug.

'Sure.'

'Come look, if you don't believe me,' Alice called after them.

'Don't pay any attention to her,' Dee whispered as she and Doug walked down the hall, hand in hand. 'There's a sweet potato in the water.'

'I know. I put it there.'

She stopped short. 'You?'

Doug nodded, whispering. 'Mr Trenton showed us how at school.'

'I thought Alice did it,' Dee admitted.

Doug grinned, his new tooth showing. 'I tricked her, huh?'

Recovering her surprise, Dee chuckled. 'You sure did.'

'It's a potato. Oh, very funny!' Alice hollered from the doorway.

Dee laughed all the way to the basement. But her pleasure in Doug's trick came to a screeching halt at the bottom of the stairs. For there was Michael, fiddling with Doug's train. One glimpse into those disheartened eyes and yesterday's hurt rushed over her again.

'Made it back from Sally's, I see.' Michael's tone belied his expression. He glanced around for Mr Kolupa, who was looking on from behind him, then back at her. 'Have a nice time?'

'What're *you* doing down here?'' she dispensed with the pleasantries.

'Taking the oxidation off the wheels of this engine,' Michael dropped the steel wool, passed the engine to Doug, and said, 'Thanks, Doug. Here, see if it doesn't work better now.'

'*Thanks, Doug?*' Dee echoed. '*You* sent him?'

'I saw you looking out the window earlier,' he admitted. 'But you didn't come over. What was I supposed to do?'

'I'm mad at you, Michael,' she told him straight out.

'I know.' He looked ashamed. 'I was pretty awful. I want to apologize. And explain, if you'll listen.'' Looking back at Grandpa again, he added in a softer voice, 'But not here. Come outside with me a minute?'

His earnest entreaty was hard to resist. Could they work this out? Or was she just setting herself up for more hurt down the road? On the tracks, the old train engine mimicked her heart's stop and go impulses.

'It's still doing it,' Doug complained.

'It's loose,' said Mr Kolupa.

Distracted, Michael suggested. 'You may have to oil the axle.'

'Dad already did that,' said Doug.

'It's loose, Michael,' said Michael's grandpa again. He leaned closer and tapped on the trans-former box.

'The wire? You're right, Grandpa.' Michael's startled expression turned to delight. He pulled a small screwdriver out of his back pocket and passed it back to his grandfather. 'Here, show Doug how to fix it.'

Mr Kolupa loosened a screw. But his hands weren't supple enough to hold the small wire in place and tighten the screw at the same time. Losing interest, he returned to screwdriver to Michael. 'It's your turn.'

Dee saw the elation on Michael's face fade to stoic resignation. It was a simple moment. But telling. *Loose connections*. What were they going to do about Mr Kolupa?

'There, try it again,' Michael motioned to Doug.

Whistle tooting, the engine chugged around the track without faltering. Doug beamed. 'Thanks.'

'You bet.'

'We're going outside for a minute. You okay with that?' Dee asked, uncertain Doug would want to be left alone in the basement with Michael's grandpa.

'I can take Grandpa home,' Michael offered.

But Doug wagged his head. 'He likes the train. Let him stay.'

Dee and Michael never made it outside. The top of the steps on the landing was far enough. Dee closed the door leading downstairs and the one ot the kitchen too. It was a small, space. That was good. No place to hide what stood between them. It was so quiet, she imagined she could hear Michael's heart beating. Or was it her own?

Fingertip in his pockets, lashes a dark smudge beneath downcast eyes, he murmured, 'I'm sorry I hurt your feelings yesterday.'

'You didn't want me there.'

'No,' he admitted. 'I didn't.'

'Why?'

'It's hard to accept him the way that he is. That he won't get any better. And that he's going to die.' He swallowed hard and added, 'If it's a downer for me, what is it for you? You know what I mean?'

'No, not exactly,' she said softly.

Struggling with himself, he let go a deep sigh. 'With all that's going on, there's days...' He stopped, ducked his head and tried again. 'I guess I get to thinking you might like to be with someone who doesn't have all this crap going on in his life. Someone more fun.'

'That's crazy!'

'Hey, I'm being honest, okay?'

Heat rushed to her face. Seemed like Alice wasn't the only critic in the family. If it was what he felt, then that was what he felt. 'All right,' she said at length. 'Thanks for telling me.'

'You're not mad any more?'

She shook her head no. 'I just want to be able to talk about things. Instead of keeping it inside. You know?'

'It's not that easy. Some of it, I won't even think about myself. I turn on the TV or the radio, and try to block it all out. Except it doesn't go away.'

'You could *try* talking about it,' she said gently. 'Couldn't you?' At length he nodded.

Encouraged, Dee reached for his hand. 'Okay, then. Let's practice.'

His fingers closed over hers. 'Practice *what*?'

She flushed at his slow, baiting grin. *Talking*.

'About what?'

'Your grandpa.'

'All right,' he said evenly. 'What do you want to know?'

'Is he home to stay?'

His fingers tightened on hers as he signed and admitted. 'That's a tough one. I don't know yet, Dee. He's cared for at Rosewood. But it isn't home. Tulip said there's guilt either way. I guess she's right.'

She withdrew a step. 'You talked to Tulip, but you wouldn't talk to me?'

'You know Tulip. She doesn't give you much choice. Besides, Dee, I'm not in love with Tulip. If

247

she thinks I'm a jerk, it's no big deal.'

Heart melting, Dee dismissed Tulip. Her thoughts skipped back to the entry she'd just read from Pru's diary. It pertained in a way to Michael, for until Miss Ellis came along, Pru had thought her choices were limited to one extreme or another. She paraphrased it as best she could for Michael. But before he could respond, the door leading up from the basement opened. It was Doug and Mr Kolupa.

'He's tired,' said Doug. 'He wants to lie down.'

'Thanks, Doug. I'll take him home,' said Michael. To Dee, he added, 'You planning on going to the fireworks later?'

She smiled, a sparkler or two shooting off inside. 'Wouldn't miss it.'

'See you about dusk then,' he said.

Doug walked out through the garage with him. But he was back in a moment. He tugged at the brim of his engineer cap and said shyly, 'I know how the dream ends.'

'What dream? Oh,' said Dee, remembering. 'Tell me.'

'Mr Kolupa was playing trains with me. He was the station-master. That's why he had my watch.'

Misunderstanding, Dee said carefully, 'You gave him your watch, Doug?'

'Well, now,' he said, as if she were dense. Pulling the gold chain from his pocket, he reminded, 'It was just a dream, Dee.'

*   *   *   *

Michael was in his room, waiting for Grandpa to drift off to sleep. Firecrackers exploded across the street. Grandpa's eyes fluttered open.

'Back-fired,' he mumbled, foot thumping.

'It's okay. You rest now.'

'Stella's waiting. Pull it up to the door.' Grandpa raised up on one elbow.

Going along with it, Michael crossed to the door.

'Go on,' said Grandpa impatiently. 'I haven't got all day.'

Michael looked back from the hallway to see Grandpa lying back on the pillow. *Was Grandma waiting?* He chose to think that she was. That Richard waited too. And others who loved Grandpa. Just as Sheri and Walt and the girls had waited to receive little Ira Earl. Waited, until the womb couldn't hold him any longer. The world he was born into was space and light and sound after months of close, dark silence. But it didn't come without trauma.

This present trauma, this darkness sucking at Grandpa – *did it precede a death or a birth?* He couldn't hold him here, no more than Ira Earl could keep from being born. Tulip had tried, with her wacky analogies, to drive that fact home. He had it now. He finally had. But it needed weight, it needed an anchor. Roots to hold on to the seed that fear could blow away. Tulip couldn't give him that, and neither could Grandpa. The road test was his. The plodding.

Michael turned the radio on low, hoping to cover the intermittent pop of firecrackers. The nurse had told him, when he picked Grandpa up that morning, that he'd been awake much of last night. He'd arranged chairs. And fed birds. And danced. Maybe he'd sleep well and awake to a blue moon. For there were blue moons. There'd been one today when the clouds cleared for an instant, and Grandpa had known about the wires.

Quietly, Michael closed the door and went out on the deck to tell Mom he was going next door to Dee's. There was plenty of time later to tell her about his decision concerning Grandpa. It'd come to him through Dee's relating her great-great-grandmother's diary entry. It didn't have to be all of one, or all of the other. Grandpa could spend his nights at Rosewood so that he and Mom would get some rest. Evenings, he'd spend at home. As for the days, they'd work them out one day at a time, through good days and bad days. And blue moons. Thank God for blue moons.